MW01131163

A Matter of Time

The Chronicles of Kerrigan Sequel, Volume 1

W.J. May

Published by Dark Shadow Publishing, 2016.

This is a work of fiction. Similarities to real people, places, or events are entirely coincidental.

A MATTER OF TIME

Also by W.J. May

Bit-Lit Series
Lost Vampire
Cost of Blood
Price of Death

Blood Red Series
Courage Runs Red
The Night Watch
Marked by Courage
Forever Night

Daughters of Darkness: Victoria's Journey
Victoria
Huntress
Coveted (A Vampire & Paranormal Romance)
Twisted

Hidden Secrets Saga
Seventh Mark - Part 1
Seventh Mark - Part 2
Marked By Destiny
Compelled
Fate's Intervention
Chosen Three
The Hidden Secrets Saga: The Complete Series

The Chronicles of Kerrigan
Rae of Hope
Dark Nebula
House of Cards

Royal Tea
Under Fire
End in Sight
Hidden Darkness
Twisted Together
Mark of Fate
Strength & Power
Last One Standing
Rae of Light
The Chronicles of Kerrigan Box Set Books # 1 - 6

The Chronicles of Kerrigan Prequel
Christmas Before the Magic
Question the Darkness
Into the Darkness
Fight the Darkness
Alone in the Darkness
Lost in Darkness

The Chronicles of Kerrigan Sequel
A Matter of Time
Time Piece

The Hidden Secrets Saga
Seventh Mark (part 1 & 2)

The Senseless Series
Radium Halos
Radium Halos - Part 2
Nonsense

The X Files
Code X
Replica X

Standalone
Shadow of Doubt (Part 1 & 2)
Five Shades of Fantasy
Glow - A Young Adult Fantasy Sampler
Shadow of Doubt - Part 2
Four and a Half Shades of Fantasy
Full Moon
Dream Fighter
What Creeps in the Night
Forest of the Forbidden
HuNted
Arcane Forest: A Fantasy Anthology
Ancient Blood of the Vampire and Werewolf

The Chronicles of Kerrigan Sequel

A Matter of Time

Book I

By

W.J. May

Copyright 2016 by W.J. May

Have You Read the C.o.K Prequel Series?

A Sub-Series of the Chronicles of Kerrigan.
A prequel on how Simon Kerrigan met Beth!!
Download for FREE:

PREQUEL –
Christmas Before the Magic
Question the Darkness
Into the Darkness
Fight the Darkness
Alone the Darkness
Lost the Darkness

The Chronicles of Kerrigan

Book I - *Rae of Hope* is FREE!
    Book Trailer:
    http://www.youtube.com/watch?v=gILAwXxx8MU
    Book II - *Dark Nebula*
    Book Trailer:
    http://www.youtube.com/watch?v=Ca24STi_bFM
    Book III - *House of Cards*
    Book IV - *Royal Tea*
    Book V - *Under Fire*
    Book VI - *End in Sight*
    Book VII – *Hidden Darkness*
    Book VIII – *Twisted Together*
    Book IX – *Mark of Fate*
    Book X – *Strength & Power*
    Book XI – *Last One Standing*
    Book XII – *Rae of Light*

PREQUEL –
Christmas Before the Magic
Question the Darkness
Into the Darkness
Fight the Darkness
Alone the Darkness
Lost the Darkness
SEQUEL –
Matter of Time
Time Piece

Find W.J. May

Website:
http://www.wanitamay.yolasite.com
Facebook:
https://www.facebook.com/pages/Author-WJ-May-FAN-PAGE/141170442608149
Newsletter:
SIGN UP FOR W.J. May's Newsletter to find out about new releases, updates, cover reveals and even freebies!
http://eepurl.com/97aYf

Description

A Matter of Time
The Chronicles of Kerrigan Sequel

The highly-anticipated sequel to the Chronicles of Kerrigan series, by international bestselling author, W.J. May

It's time.

The past can't stay buried forever...

Rae Kerrigan and her friends thought all their problems were solved. The corruption in the Council has been exposed. The hybrids have been released from their unjust prisons. And Jonathon Cromfield—the evil puppet master pulling all the strings—has finally been put in the ground.

With the promise of an actual future with Devon, the love of her life, Rae slips the ring back onto her finger and turned her eyes towards the horizon. Her heart's filled with hope.

Except, fate has other plans...

With the return of her father, the infamous Simon Kerrigan who started it all, Rae finds that her newly right world has turned upside down again. The new peace in the tatù realm has shattered once more. Turning friends against friends. Family against family.

Why was he imprisoned? What will he do now? More importantly, can Simon Kerrigan ever be trusted again?

Rae and her team intend to find out...

Chapter 1

'Lost time is never found again.'

Benjamin Franklin

But sometimes, just sometimes, you can find the things time left behind in its shadow.

It can't be.

It was as if the room itself had turned to stone, rendering everyone in it a frozen statue; eyes wide with fear and astonishment, unable to believe it could be true. The only movement that broke through the stillness was a quiet shuffling—the sounds of two unsteady feet slowly making their way towards the light.

"Beth?"

All the blue dilated out of Rae's eyes as she took an automatic step back. Her shoulder blades pressed into Devon's chest, standing just behind her, but she took no comfort in his presence. His pulse was as frantic and scattered as hers.

This...cannot be happening. This has to be a dream.

The man took another uncertain step forward—wincing at the light leaking in from the hallway, as if even its meager shine was enough to do him harm. He lifted his hand halfway in front of his face, shielding his eyes as he tried to speak again. "B-Beth...is that you?"

The sound of his voice attacked Rae from all sides. Swooping down on her like a thousand vicious spirits. A thousand terrible memories she thought had been forever laid to rest.

She didn't answer. Couldn't speak. The idea never even occurred to her. Her every thought was dominated by one single command, one single chance to leave this all behind her.

Run.

But her feet wouldn't move. Neither would Devon's. Neither would any of the twelve armed men they'd brought with them to clear the dungeons. It was as if they were all under the same ghastly spell. Watching, completely incapacitated, as the man of their nightmares came slowly forth.

"That's..." An elderly guard standing with the rest of the contingent covered his mouth with a shaking hand. A weather-hardened soldier to be sure, but he had suddenly met his match. "That's Simon Kerrigan."

The name sent out a shockwave, rippling through the little cavern and echoing against its the walls.

Simon Kerrigan.

Although Rae had grown up trapped under the legacy of that name, although she had grown up fighting the weight of it with everything she had...it was like she was hearing it for the first time.

Her eyes flashed up and rested for a split second on his face. A face that had stared up at her from archived 'wanted' posters and open homicide investigations for the better part of her life. A face that should have been a stranger, but somehow was as familiar as her own.

Their eyes met in the darkness. Father and daughter, standing there for the first time. The entire world seemed to stop turning, and for a moment it was just the two of them.

Then the weight of reality came crashing down upon them, leaving a trail of unimaginable panic and years of devastation smoking in its wake.

"No..." Devon's hands wrapped around her upper arms, pulling her protectively against his chest. "No, that's not...that couldn't be..."

But Simon seemed to notice Devon at the same time. For a moment his bleary eyes went wide with wonder, then he took another halting step forward. "Tristan?"

Devon's entire body locked down. Pressed up against him, Rae could feel it just as easily as if they'd been standing face to face. His lips parted, but not a whisper of sound came out. For a moment, he simply stood there—just as lost as she.

Then all at once, the entire cavern sprang to life.

At some unseen signal, a dozen hammers were cocked. A dozen guards lifted their guns in perfect unison—pointing each one at Simon Kerrigan's chest.

Simon froze where he stood. His eyes flickered over Rae and Devon, stricken in the center of the room, before he took a faltering step back.

"I'm sorry..." His voice was hoarse from lack of use. "I wasn't trying to..."

The room fell silent again. Twelve fingers poised on the trigger. Not a single breath among them. A man's entire life coming down to a single moment in time.

"Just awaiting your orders, Madame President."

While the title still felt strange to Rae's ears, Simon looked up in surprise. Surprise that turned to genuine pride and affection as he recognized the face of his daughter for the first time.

"You're the President of the Privy Council." Despite the darkness around them, his eyes softened with a paternal glow. "Rae."

If hearing Simon's name had stopped her heart, hearing her own name brought Rae back to life. He might have set fire to her past, but she had risen from the ashes to give herself a new future.

She wasn't about to let all that slip away now. Not for anything. Certainly not for this.

All her years of training and experience suddenly came rushing back, steadying her shaking hands and silencing that ominous ringing in her ears. The legendary fairy painted on her lower back hummed with anticipation, ready to bring any of a hundred active powers bursting forth.

And all the pain, and loss, and sacrifice...still fresh beneath the surface from a battle's devastating cost, unlocked her frozen body. Propelling her forward into the cell.

"Rae..."

While Simon had said her name as an affirmation, Devon said it as a quiet plea. A warning for caution. There were no tatùs within these walls, but they had all grown up hearing enough stories of Simon Kerrigan to believe in the myth as well as the man.

He took a step with her, unwilling to let her go too far. On either side of them, the contingent of guards followed suit their guns still raised at the ready.

After 'the battle to save the world', as it had been quickly named by some of the younger members of the inked generation, the power dynamics within the society's upper echelons had irrevocably shifted. Not only had Rae been unanimously asked to assume the presidency of the Privy Council, but she and her friends had been forcibly thrust into a position of near-royalty. A cult of fervent veneration had sprung up around the young friends. A respect bordering almost upon reverence that elevated their already-renowned story to the stuff of legends.

It was a strange and unwelcome position to find themselves in, seeing as the only thing the reluctant heroes wanted to do at the moment was shut themselves away from the world and cry. It also meant that, even though Rae and Devon were undoubtedly the most formidable warriors in the cell, their own guard felt absurdly protective of them.

The second Devon stepped forward, three hands shot out to pull him back. They would have done the same thing with Rae if she wasn't already halfway across the floor, standing face to face with her father.

Would you look at that...

He was tall. She'd never known that before. With a beard that spoke to almost two decades kept in captivity. In all the pictures she'd seen, he'd always been clean-shaven.

She tilted her head and leaned in closer still.

It probably wasn't wise to get so close. If she hadn't figured that out herself, she could always pick up on it from the palpable tension coming from her people on the other side of the room. No, it probably wasn't wise. But what part of this situation possibly made sense?

The man was dead.

There was a death certificate to prove it. There were a dozen eye-witnesses to back it up. She had seen it herself, for Pete's sake. She had seen the kitchen ceiling give way. Seen the waves of liquid fire crash down upon his head. He had been buried in rubble, only to emerge a broken corpse, not a flicker of life left in his body.

And yet...

Her blue eyes traced him up and down, taking in every little detail with spellbound attention, only to realize that he was doing the exact same thing to her. Their eyes met in the middle, and for a second she was almost tempted to reach out and touch him. If only to make sure that he was real.

Then Devon's voice cracked out like a whip. *"Kerrigan!"*

Both Rae and Simon looked up at the same time.

She glanced over her shoulder, lingering a moment on her fiancé's anxious face before returning to her father's. That same paternal smile was still lighting him up, quickening his breath, before settling in his eyes as he beamed down at her.

"You look so much like your mother."

Rae blinked once.

Then she pulled back her fist, and knocked him right to the floor.

A dozen frantic whispers echoed nervously off the cell walls, creating a low buzz in Rae's ears as she stared down at her father. For his part, Simon Kerrigan was sleeping peacefully on the stone floor, completely oblivious to the fact that his own flesh and blood had just punched him with enough force to dent a car.

"—can't believe that's actually him. They buried him, didn't they? Had a funeral?"

"Cremated, I think. No funeral. Because who the hell would go?"

"But that's Simon, alright. I was a few years above him in school. The beard threw me for a second, but I'd know him anywhere. There are some faces you just can't hide..."

There are some faces you just can't hide.

Rae stared down at Simon, ignoring the chaos going on around her as she pondered the wisdom in those words.

Was it true? Were there some things so terrible, that no matter how deep you buried them in the ground they would always come back up to haunt you? Could you only run so far before the past eventually caught up?

Several minutes passed, but Rae found that she couldn't move a muscle. All she could do was stare. The buzzing in her ears grew louder and more impatient, but still she stayed right where she was, kneeling over Simon's fallen body. Staring at his closed eyes, as if at any moment they could snap open and drop her where she stood.

As usual, Devon was just a step behind. He, too, had remained perfectly still. A far cry from his usual perpetual motion, but the boy was a perfect statue. The only time he moved was to reach out and grab someone's cell phone, crumbling it in his hand before it could complete the call.

"Wait...please."

The guards instantly complied with his soft-spoken request. But the buzzing remained.

An obvious question floated to the forefront of everyone's mind, echoed back in a dozen different voices, phrased a dozen different ways. And the longer they stood there, the longer they talked, the more that question demanded an answer.

What the hell are we going to do?

"Rae," Devon finally broke the unending stalemate. While she had been staring at Simon, he was only staring at her. "We need to make a move here."

But Rae was lost, staring down at her father with a contemplative tilt to her head. "We have the same mouth, don't you think?" Her hair spilled to the side as she examined him further. "I never noticed it before," she murmured, "but look. It's so obvious."

A look of mild panic flitted across Devon's face, but he was quick to keep it in check. He placed a gentle hand on her shoulder, but instead of pulling her up to her feet he sank down so that they were side by side—staring at the problem together.

"Honey," he murmured, soft enough that only she could hear, "we can't just stay."

No. We can't just stay.

Another obvious truth. Another layer to the problem.

But...what's the alternative?

That, it turned out, was the real question.

Like a person coming out of a deep sleep Rae glanced behind her at the circle of guards, all of them still pointing their semi-automatics right at Simon's chest. There was a distinct vigilance to the way they were standing—protective, because she was so close—but there was something else there as well. A deep hatred. One that knew no limits or bounds. They would shoot him right here as he slept. No qualms. No remorse.

...and would that be so wrong?

The man was supposed to be dead. He had killed countless people. Performed unspeakable torture. Ruined countless lives.

And yet...

"Devon," her voice dropped to a shaking whisper, "I can't—"

"President Kerrigan."

The two of them fell instantly quiet as Mitchell Ford, the acting head of security for both the Council and the school, knelt respectfully by their side. A part of Rae was desperate for him to leave so they could talk in peace. Another part was grateful he'd brought his gun.

"I understand this is a shock, and an impossible situation you find yourself in." His voice carried just the hint of a Southern drawl, but every part of him was solid. Compact. A moving mass of muscle paired with a rational mind that made him perfect for the job. "And after the ordeal you and Mr. Wardell have been through, no one could expect you to make this decision on your own..." he paused for a moment, and Rae looked up into his eyes, "...so let me."

For a moment, the two of them just stared.

Is he saying what I think he's saying?

Beside her, Devon's lips parted in surprise. But he looked neither eager to accept the offer nor eager to turn it down. He was somewhere in the middle.

For her part Rae simply turned back to Simon, unable to formulate a single response.

Ford saw his opportunity and gently pressed forward.

"Simon Kerrigan is a murderer who deserves to die. There's no other way of looking at it. Now, he is technically still your father, and I understand why that might impede your ability to make this sort of call."

He straightened up slightly, looking like he was on the verge of a salute.

"Rest assured...it will not impede mine."

Rae tore her eyes away from her sleeping father and gazed up at the man. A man who she had come to like very much the last few days, given the circumstances. He was logical, pragmatic, focused, and kind. An unlikely combination for any one person to have, and one that made him an invaluable asset to their protection force. An asset whose opinion she happened to value very much.

And here he was suggesting...

"Thanks, Mitch," Devon cut in quickly, sensing she'd reached her limit. "Just give us a second to work it out."

The man nodded, and swiftly got to his feet. But before he did so, he reached out and squeezed Rae's arm with what he obviously thought to be words of comfort.

"It'll be painless. I'll make it quick. More than he deserves."

Rae let out a quiet gasp as he returned to the ranks, wishing desperately—more than she had ever wished before—that she could simply sink into Devon's arms. Close her eyes. Not have to think about this. Not be called upon to make this kind of decision.

As if on cue, a throat cleared softly and the guards turned discreetly to the side. They were still watching, of course, but also allowing their charges as much privacy as was possible.

Devon glanced back at them quickly before slipping his arm around Rae's shoulders. One hand came up over the side of her face as he cradled her softly against his chest. "I'll do whatever you want," he murmured into her hair. "Whatever you think is best."

Whatever I think is best?! Do I think it's best to execute my father by firing squad?!

Well... maybe.

A wracking shudder shook Rae's entire frame but, no matter what, she found herself unable to cry. Instead, she kept her eyes trained on Simon. Trying to imagine if the world would be a better place without him in it. Trying to imagine if it was a guilt she could possibly survive.

What would Carter do?

And just like that, as quickly as the question had arisen, it was forever laid to rest.

"I just lost one father," she said in a low voice, "and now you're asking me to shoot the other one in the head?"

Another shudder rippled through her, but she shook her head.

"I can't do that."

With a sudden flood of determination, she silently pushed to her feet... Devon right by her side. If her decision was badly received by the guards—and with Simon's reputation, how could it not be—they were well-disciplined enough not to show it. And it was a good thing, too. Because she had made another decision, one that would put their loyalty to the test.

"I'm going to ask something of you now, each and every one of you." She stared around the silent circle, looking each man in the eyes before moving on to the next. "I want you to keep this to yourselves, at least...for a little while. Until I make a more permanent decision as to what to do."

This time, her request was met with restless shifting. Darting eyes. Discontent.

"I understand exactly what it means to ask this," she continued carefully, forbidding herself to glance at Devon at the risk of what she might see. "I understand exactly the risk. But let me assure you, gentlemen, and this is a promise: no one here has more cause to hate Simon Kerrigan than me."

The shifting stopped. The men were focused once more.

"I'm going to assume full responsibility for him. He'll be under my constant supervision until such time as I see fit. I don't have to tell you what that means..."

No, she didn't. After the recent events that had taken place in this very factory, there wasn't a single person of ink who wouldn't trust her with their lives. To say that Simon would be under Rae's supervision was almost better than to say that he'd be locked away in some cage.

"I don't want to make it an order," she said softly, locking eyes with Ford, "but I will if I have to. No one knows about this, understood?"

"Understood!"

The men echoed it back in a chorus, no one louder than their fearless leader. He met Rae's eye with a solemn nod, and inclined his head.

"And no, Miss Kerrigan...you don't need to make it an order."

A ghost of a smile flitted across her face, and she nodded gratefully. "Thank you. All of you."

Simon stirred on the ground beneath them, and time was suddenly of the essence.

"Now go," she commanded, gesturing to the door. "Leave one of the cars for Devon andme to take back. The one with the containment hold in the back. Should anyone ask—we found nothing. There was nothing in the cells."

The men's eyes flickered again to Simon, but came to rest on both Rae and Devon—angled strategically in front—and were reassured. At least for now.

They backed away with a parting salute and disappeared back up the tunnels, leaving Rae and Devon in a suddenly awkward silence in the cell.

He turned back to her slowly, weighing each word before he said them, trying his best to be supportive when he clearly thought she had just lost her mind. "Rae, honey...help me out here."

"I know, I know." She threw up her hands, the professional façade falling away the second the two of them were alone in the room. "It was rash, and impulsive, and unbelievably freaking stupid. I just...Devon, I just couldn't let them kill him right there on the floor." She shook her head, feeling suddenly lost. "He's my father."

Devon's face tightened painfully at the heartbroken look on hers, wanting desperately to make their every problem vanish.

But the fact still remained. "I understand that," he said softly. "I'm glad you stopped them. But..." His eyes drifted nervously over Simon's body, still unable to believe he was real, "I thought the only two options were Mitch's offer, or imprisonment until trial. Rae...what do you mean you're going to assume full responsibility for him? You're just going to leave him here in the cell?"

"No." Rae shook her head quickly, planning on the spot. "We can't leave him in the cell. I trust the men completely, but the factory is public property. Without Cromfield's protections over the place, there's no telling who might wander in and find him. No," she took a deep breath, "he'll have to be moved."

Devon nodded slowly, trying desperately to follow along. "Okay...and where exactly do you want to move him?"

Please, oh please—love of my life, soulmate and friend, my future husband—please don't hate me for what I'm about to say next.

"I was thinking in the boathouse...?"

Chapter 2

After the tragic battle and their unfortunate rise to celebrity, Rae's circle of friends had needed to leave it all behind. To hole themselves away somewhere private, a place where they could lick their wounds and grieve their losses. If only for a little while.

Despite their ringleader's election as President of the Privy Council, the rest of them had vanished completely off the grid—taking an indefinite leave of absence at a shared house they'd bought in the countryside, a house to which both Rae and Devon were both eager to return. This cursory 'clearing of the factory' had been the last official event Rae was bound to perform for the next several weeks. It was supposed to be quick. Painless.

But, as usual...fate had other plans.

"The boathouse? Are you insane?" Devon exclaimed, losing his cool for a moment.

Yep, it pretty much looks that way.

She raised her hands peaceably. "I know how it sounds—"

"—it sounds like you want to stash your lunatic father in our boathouse." Devon followed her pointed gaze back down to Simon, throwing up his hands. "Oh, I'm sorry, what do you want me to call him? Mr. Kerrigan? Dear old Dad?"

"We can't just leave him here—"

"And we can't just hide him in the boathouse, Rae! He's not a puppy!"

Simon stirred on the floor between them, and for a moment they fell quiet, just watching. After a second, he rolled to the side and moved no more.

"Yeah," Rae gritted her teeth, "I'm pretty clear on that. Thanks."

Devon sighed, running his hands back through his hair the way he did when he was either on the verge of hyperventilating or a full-on mental breakdown. At this point, it was probably both.

"I'm sorry, I didn't mean to yell. It's just..." He glanced back down at Simon, a rather helpless expression washing over his face. "Rae, we're in over our heads here. This isn't the kind of secret you can keep, and it's certainly not the kind of secret you can keep in our boathouse."

"Why not?" Rae asked desperately, well aware that she was grasping at straws. "There's no boat in it. It's just sitting there. Right on the property. Right under our watch."

"Right by the house where all of our *friends* are staying?"

His silent accusation fell on deaf ears as she began nodding quickly, getting more and more swept up in her plan. "You're right. They can never know. This isn't something that involves them."

Devon's mouth fell open in dismay. "Isn't something that...?! Rae, that's not what I was saying at all! Of *course* this involves them! Especially if you want to bring him home!"

But on this point Rae was resolute. Completely unwilling to budge. "Really? And how would you suggest we tell them, Devon? Think about it."

The tiny cell fell silent once more as a silent roster of faces flashed through their minds.

Each one in recovery and retreat. Each one clinging to every passing moment with shaking hands, just trying to keep themselves together.

Devon faltered, unwilling to imagine shattering the fragile calm they'd worked so hard to build.

Rae saw her moment, and pressed forward. "Molly?" she asked softly. "Pregnant at eight weeks? You want to tell her that our final battle didn't mean anything after all? That a new catastrophe just walked through our door?"

Devon bit his lip, and remained silent.

"Julian?" she continued, watching him speculatively. "I just found out that my father is actually alive...and Julian didn't even call. Want to know why? Because he didn't see it. He isn't watching. He's keeping himself right there in the present. With Angel. With all of us. And who the hell can blame him, after everything we've been through."

"Rae..." Devon pressed his fingers against his temples, closing his eyes. "Stop."

"My mother."

His eyes snapped open, and for a moment the two of them just stared at each other.

Beth had not been the same since Carter's death.

She still put together a funeral. Still showed up at Rae's inauguration. Still answered the phone when she was called. But the movements were robotic. Not a spark of life behind them. Not a single thing to indicate that there was an actual person in there. Someone capable of being happy.

Of course, the loss was so recent no one really expected anything different. But Beth's detachment was something deeper than that. It was something permanent.

She had waited a *lifetime* for Carter. Loved him from the moment she knew what love really was. Married him on the cliffs at sunset.

...and then buried him ten days later.

"No," Devon said quietly, after an unending moment of time, "we can't tell your mom."

"If we leave him here, he'll be found," Rae spoke rapidly now, her voice soft with the power of persuasion. "If we turn him in, they'll murder him before he gets a fair trial. The only solution is to take him someplace where he can't hurt anyone. And not to brag, but you and I both know that the safest place in the whole world is with the two of us."

Devon stared down at the still form, his features twisting with bitter dislike. "So, he can only hurt the two of us?"

Rae bit her lip to stifle a grin. Worries about self-harm weren't Devon's style. He was just stalling now. She had him. "Come on, you big baby. What's he going to do? Hit you with his beard?" She shoved him playfully to coax a smile. "He looks like he just escaped from the set of *Castaway*. I think we can take him."

Devon grinned at her teasing, but his face sobered up in a hurry when they both stared back down at Simon, considering the next logistical steps. "We don't know what kind of tatù he's carrying," he warned softly, glancing down at Simon's hands like they were likely to explode. "And no matter what it is, the boathouse isn't equipped to contain ink like this place is."

Rae glanced at the stone walls with a worried frown. He had a point. The only way to ensure that a man like Simon could do no harm was to put him in a place that would permanently disable his tatù. And the only place she knew of that could do that were the secret dungeons beneath the Oratory of the Privy Council. And the only way *they* were even able to do it was by using...

"Honey?" She took Devon's hand with a sweet smile. "How would you feel about making a little stop along the way?"

"I cannot *believe* I let you talk me into this."

Rae sped nervously down the country road, heading towards her old school. In the backseat Devon was keeping a nervous eye on the trunk, making sure it didn't burst open in a spray of fire and brimstone that was sure to end them all.

"What?" She forced a laugh, trying to lighten the mood. "The whole my dad thing? Or the fact that you're letting me drive the company car?"

'Letting' was putting it nicely. The second they'd carried Simon to the curb—wrapped in Devon's coat like a straitjacket so he wouldn't touch their skin—he had commanded that she be the one sitting behind the wheel. This freed him up for prisoner watch. A responsibility he was taking very seriously, as he hadn't lifted his eyes from the window even once in the last hour.

His eyes narrowed into a glare in the reflection of the glass. "How about the fact that we're driving straight into Privy Council Headquarters, with Simon Kerrigan himself lying in the trunk."

Rae bit her lip, and aimed for the bright side. "At least he's tied up—"

"In my *coat*, Rae! He's tied up in my *jacket*!" He actually turned around for a moment to glare up at her through the cab. "Such a shame they didn't think of that all those years ago. Found his fatal weakness. Fleece."

She pulled herself up a little straighter, eyes sharpening up as they exited the freeway onto more familiar ground. "He's out cold. I hit him again just to be sure, and he's temporarily frozen with Angel's tatù. He's not going anywhere."

Devon flashed her a look, but said not a word as they pulled quickly up to the guard gate of their old school. He didn't have to.

The message was clear.

You'd better be right.

"I forgot some paperwork, and you're fast asleep," Rae muttered hastily as she pulled to a stop. The window was already rolling down, but Devon didn't need to be told twice. The second she said the words he slid down in the seat, closing his eyes as he leaned up against the window.

"Evening, Charlie," Rae said with a smile as she put the car in park.

The young man sitting behind the desk hurried forward, both nervous and excited to be talking to such an illustrious visitor. "Good evening, President Kerrigan!"

Rae flinched. "Charlie, we've been through this about a hundred times. I'm, like, four years older than you. Will you please call me Rae?"

"Not a chance, President Kerrigan," he said with a grin, glancing back to see Devon resting his head against the glass. "Late night?"

Rae glanced back casually before tossing him another smile. "A couple of late nights, actually. I can't believe how much paperwork comes with this job you all foisted on me. I actually left some in my office and that's why we're swinging by."

"Oh, no problem." He hurried to open the gate, bowing his head politely as she sped on through. "I'll just...leave it open for you then?"

"Thanks, Charlie!" she called as they shot off down the drive.

The second they were out of sight, Devon slowly lifted his head. The moonlit trees and familiar scenery did nothing to soothe his nerves. If anything, he felt even more apprehensive to have brought such a dangerous criminal within the walls of the school.

"He likes you."

Rae glanced back in the mirror with a frown. "What?"

"Charlie. He likes you."

She snorted and shook her head. "Charlie's a sixteen-year-old boy. He likes everything that happens to walk and have breasts at the same time."

Devon grinned faintly out the window. "It's more than that. He's got a serious crush."

Rae glanced back once more, bewildered as to why they were having such a trivial conversation in light of heavier things. Then Devon flashed a hint of those adorable dimples, and she realized that fixating on a trivial conversation to distract from such things may have been exactly the point.

"I guess we'll just see where it goes." She shrugged causally. "I've been framing his poems, answering his letters...trying to keep an open mind."

"You should loan him some of your shoes," Devon replied lightly. "It's the only way he'll even come close to your height. You know, if there's going to be kissing involved..."

"You'd like that, wouldn't you?" she said flatly, aiming for the parking space nearest to the Oratory door. "Getting Charlie all dressed up like that. Maybe he's not the only one who's got a little crush."

At this, Devon laughed out loud. But he stopped quickly as the car came to a stop and she shut off the engine. They both stared at the door for a moment before she turned around with a little sigh.

Rae inhaled deeply. "Are you sure you just don't want to run in and get it? You're the one who knows what it looks like."

There was not an inch of compromise on Devon's face. "Not a chance in hell. I'm staying here with him. If he wakes up...you're not going to be anywhere close, do you hear me?"

She rolled her eyes and stifled another sigh. "Fine. Just tell me again where it is."

"There's a supply closet, just next to the back-up power generator." Her face blanked, and it was his turn to roll his eyes. "Next to the picture of that guy you always say looks like a ferret."

Rae nodded in a moment of illumination. "Oh, right."

"Inside, there's a whole box. It's not exactly proprietary technology, so they're pretty casual about storing it. A tiny, metallic triangle. That's what it's going to look like."

"Got it." She slipped out without another word, moving quickly towards her destination. But halfway there, she suddenly turned back around. Devon met her eyes through the back window, frowning a question as she stopped just a few feet in front of the door. She pulled in a deep breath, then pressed her fingers against her lips, mouthing two words: 'Thank you.'

His eyes softened as his lips pulled up into a gentle smile. Even through the tinting, even from a distance, she saw as clear as day when he mouthed back, 'Anytime.'

Then there was no more time to waste. The next second, she was opening the door.

Thirty minutes later, they were flying down another country road, speeding beneath the stars as Rae searched ahead for their exit. The 'tatù-inhibitors' had been just as easy to find as Devon had predicted, and since she had been technically voted in charge of the place no one paid her the slightest bit of attention as she unlocked the door with a master key and took everything she needed.

She had ended up getting three. One would do it, Devon had said. But she wasn't taking any chances. Considering the current situation, she had been down-playing her own fear. Trying to convince herself that, should the time come, she would be both able and willing to do whatever it took to restrain her father.

But, truth be told, she wasn't sure if either one of those things was true. As much as Rae Kerrigan had become an underground legend overnight—Simon was the original. There was a reason that his very name struck fear into the hearts of the masses. There was a reason that he had been able to go free as long as he had.

The man was simply unbeatable.

WAS unbeatable. Past tense. But that's all he is, and that's where he belongs. The past. I'd like to see him even try anything in front of me or Devon.

The confident voice convinced her until she spotted the house up ahead and pulled down the long gravel driveway. The second she saw the boathouse, it completely died.

No. I wouldn't like to see that at all.

All the lights were on, though it was already past midnight. The golden glow leaked out of the windows, spilling out across the grassy lawn with a false sense of cheer. Rae glanced up at the pillared doors with a sigh. *False* cheer was right. The painted smiles and forced calm her friends put on might fool the rest of the world, but she knew better.

Chances were, they had all already gone to bed. The lights were all on simply because none of them could sleep in the darkness.

She flipped off the headlights as they approached, and they rolled to a slow stop behind the cover of the boathouse. When they'd first started searching for their countryside retreat, the only criteria were that it was isolated and big enough to fit all of them. It wasn't until the boys saw the option with the boathouse that they realized they needed a place to put all their cars.

"Alright," she whispered, glancing nervously up at the house, "are you ready?"

Devon followed her gaze, his bright eyes clouding as they fixed on Julian's window.

"Rae...are you sure we can't just tell them? They're going to find out soon enough anyway, and if he's going to be staying so close they have more than a right to know." His foot tapped nervously in place just thinking of it. "I'm surprised Jules hasn't come out here already."

"But he hasn't," Rae said firmly. "Because he can't. None of them can. Not right now, Devon. They need time, you know that. They can't handle something like this. Not after everything that's happened."

He tore his eyes away from the house and met her stare in the mirror. "This feels a lot like the time you didn't tell me before running into a huge fight. When you made the decision for the both of us and left me behind, to protect me."

Rae's chest tightened. Yes, it did feel an awful lot like that time. In fact, she could almost hear the screaming arguments that were sure to come.

For now, at least for tonight, they would keep this between themselves. They only had so long before this bomb eventually went off. She was determined to shield her friends from the blast of it for as long as possible.

"Let's just get him inside, okay?" she said quietly, slipping from the car. When he hesitated, she opened his door and took him by the hand. "Devon...please."

Their eyes met for a moment before he nodded. The next second, they were circling around to the trunk, gazing down at it with frightful apprehension.

"What are we going to do if he jumps out?" Rae asked quietly. "I've never tried to keep up Angel's ink for so long before. I'm sure it wore off the second I stepped inside the Oratory."

She had been trying so hard to hold it all together, especially because Devon wasn't exactly on board with her not-so-brilliant plan. But now that the moment was staring them in the face, she found herself suddenly terrified.

His hand slipped into hers.

"If he jumps out, then you get out of the way and let me take it." His face was stern and his voice carried a serious warning. "I'm serious, Rae. Don't try to do anything brave. If he takes my power, you still have all of yours to stop him. If he gets his hands on you...there's no telling what he might be able to do."

She nodded quickly, biting down hard on her lip. Just another terrible glitch in an already terribly thought out idea. Just another terrible outcome she couldn't bring herself to think about.

"Hey," his fingers squeezed hers, and she looked up to see a reassuring smile, "chances are he's not even awake. The man's been living in a cave for almost fifteen years, and I've sparred with you enough times to know that you throw a mean right hook. Just take a breath. It'll be fine."

"Right." She nodded quickly. "It'll be fine. He's probably not even awake."

Devon gave her a swift kiss on the lips, and they both braced in the gravel. Then, before either one of them could change their minds, he pulled open the trunk.

Simon Kerrigan was smiling back at them.

Devon and Rae gasped at the same time.

Simon kept smiling. "So...is this the part where I'm supposed to jump out and yell *boo*?"

Chapter 3

The trunk lid slammed back down again. Rae and Devon leapt away as if they'd been burned.

"*Crap!*" she whispered, clutching her hair. "*Crap! Crap! Crap!*"

Devon had started pacing back and forth, his feet blurring with speed on the gravel drive while his eyes stayed fixed upon the car. "This...we can't...we can't do this."

"*Crap! Freakin' crap!*"

"This is crazy! We can't...this can't be happening right now."

"Devon, he's awake!"

The pacing stopped. A pair of strong hand grabbed her shoulders. "Yeah, genius. *I saw that he's awake*!"

Rae nodded quickly, sensing a bit of an accusation. Perhaps it was the look on his face. Or the fact that he'd somehow screamed it in a hushed undertone. "Okay, well...it's going to be alright," she began tentatively. "We're just going to—"

"No, Rae! We can't do this!" He sank into a crouch, covering his mouth with his hands as he stared helplessly at the back of the car. "We kidnapped *Simon Kerrigan*. We put him in a trunk."

It was the first time he had ever said 'Kerrigan' like all the others. Like the name alone had the power to completely debilitate and destroy. It was strange, hearing it come from his mouth. He had always been detached, pragmatic. From the time he told her about her father's unfortunate legacy on the steps of Guilder, to when they were hunting down the missing pieces of his brainwashing device. There was a sadness there, a raw resentment for what he'd done. But it was so far in the past it had never mattered much, and he kept himself above it for Rae.

Now, it seemed, the past had caught up with them. And there was something new in his voice when he said the name. Something new in his eyes when he stared at the car. Something Rae had never seen there before.

Fear.

"Dev," she tried to force herself to be calm, "it's just a regular prisoner transfer. It's something that you've done about a thousand times."

His brown eyes flashed as they tore themselves away from the car and fixed on her. "Yeah, except he's not just a regular prisoner, is he?" His fingers raked manically back through his hair, standing the dark locks on end. "Rae, I honestly don't know what's worse: That he's Simon Kerrigan, or that he's your..." He trailed off, unable to say the word.

Rae said it for him. "My father?" She was surprised by how strong her voice sounded. How suddenly calm.

Yes, he was her father. But he was also the most dangerous sociopath to walk the inked streets since the time of King Henry VIII. Well, him and Cromfield. She would not confuse the line.

And while he might be *Simon Kerrigan*...she was still *Rae*. There was a reason she had been elected to govern those streets. There was a reason people no longer looked at her like a pariah simply because of her bloodline. There was a reason people had started to love, not fear, the name.

"Set up the inhibitors," she instructed, leveling the car with her gaze. "Remember to do it on the outside, so he can't tear them down."

Devon stared at her for another second, but it helped that she had given him a task. Without another word, he silently moved forward and grabbed the bag from the car. He disappeared around the back of the boathouse, and a moment later rejoined her by the trunk. The bag was empty.

"Done," he breathed, gazing down with a forced steadiness. If there was one thing that could inspire bravery in him above everything else, it was the prospect of keeping Rae safe. He certainly didn't disappoint tonight. "Are you ready?"

She nodded, and the two of them braced in the gravel again. Ready for round two.

The trunk lifted for a second time.

Simon pursed his lips, looking like he was trying very hard not to smile. "Much better," he congratulated quietly. "The expressions, the defensive stance. I don't feel like I have a shot in hell of getting out of here. Truly."

Devon's back stiffened, and for a moment it looked like he was considering slamming the lid down again and pushing the car into the pond. Rae stepped forward instead with a tight smile.

"You'll have to excuse us. Finding you...*alive*..." She hesitated, staring back at him with uncertain eyes, the false bravado melting away in the chilled night air. "...we weren't expecting it."

For a moment, all the games and witty banter disappeared. Simon stared back at her with a rather thoughtful expression, lingering on her face before nodding his head slowly.

"The fire." His voice was still weak and scratchy from his time in captivity. "I remember there was a fire. You, your mother, the rest of the world...had to think I was gone."

And good riddance.

For a moment, the three of them just froze there. Two of them standing, one of them sitting in the trunk with a designer trench coat still wrapped clumsily around his hands.

Then, in perhaps the most frightening moment to happen yet, Simon's entire face lit up with a beaming, anticipatory smile. "Well...surprise."

The trunk door went down again.

Both Rae and Devon had done it at the same moment, so it was impossible to either take credit or place blame. As it was they both stood just in front of it, resting a shaking hand on top should he try to escape.

"How do we get him from here to the boathouse?" Devon asked softly.

Rae's mind raced as she tried to come up with a safe plan. It's not like he was going to go quietly. And it's not like they could risk letting the man touch the skin of either of them.

"You know," a muffled voice echoed out from the car, "I could always just walk there."

Rae and Devon shared a quick glance before his fist slammed down upon the trunk. A momentary loss of control, and a fierce warning for silence.

There was a brief pause. Then,

"...I bet that was the boy, wasn't it?"

Devon's face paled, and he turned back to Rae in quiet desperation. Twice his eyes flickered up to the house, as if at any moment he might yell at the top of his lungs and the rest of their super-gang would come running. Twice Rae punched him in the shoulder to make him wait.

Finally, she leaned her face down as close to the metal as she dared, considering all her options for a moment, before taking a brave stab at honesty. "Simon," she couldn't bring herself to call him 'Dad', "we don't know what tatù you're carrying. We can't risk just letting you out."

Devon flashed her a quick look, but he, too, stared down at the car. Waiting for an answer.

Simon's voice was calm and steady. Ringing with the kind of unquestionable sincerity Rae was sure he had used to get so many unsuspecting followers onto his side. "The last set of ink I took before the fire was wind. I haven't been able to use it in my cell, of course, but I'm assuming it's still intact. That's the only one."

That's the only one.

On this point, at least, Rae did believe him. Over the years she had studied the life and times of Simon Kerrigan like a dark obsession, tracking down every bit of information she could get her hands on. All with the vain hope of understanding him just a little better. Trying to come to terms with how the man her mother fell in love with turned into the monster he'd become.

Throughout the collection of this research, one fact had remained consistent.

Simon Kerrigan could use one set of ink at a time. It's the reason that everyone had been so impressed with her ability to possess multiple powers. It was the reason they had been so scared.

"Prove it." The trunk door opened a crack. Devon took a step back, pushing Rae discreetly out of Simon's line of sight as he did so. "On me."

Simon sat up tentatively, moving slowly so as not to alarm. Once the lid was fully open he glanced down at his hands, eyes lingering on the hastily knotted jacket on top.

"Do you want me to just take this off, or shall we maintain the illusion?"

Devon's face whitened another shade, but he gritted his teeth. "Just do it."

In a flash, the jacket fell to the side. Then, moving with a speed that seemed impossible given his time trapped underground, Simon lifted his hand and pointed it straight at Devon's head.

Rae sucked in a silent scream, but her man held steady. His brown eyes pierced the night as they locked onto Simon. His chest rose and fell with rapid, shallow breaths, but he surrendered not an inch of ground, staring back at the man who, in a perfect world, would be his father-in-law.

Simon's face softened a fraction of an inch, and he smiled. Then, with what looked like the utmost care, he curved his fingers in a delicate circle. The air around Devon's face began to shimmer and his dark hair danced across his forehead, blowing back in a gentle breeze. A second later, it was over. No harm. No foul.

Both Rae and Devon relaxed their shoulders with twin sighs of relief.

"Was that satisfactory?" Simon asked, peering around the corner of the car so he could see Rae as well. "Shall we proceed to this... boathouse?"

It took twenty-seven steps to get from the car to the boathouse. Just half a minute if you were walking quickly, but without a doubt it was the longest thirty seconds of Rae's life.

Even though he was clearly shaken to the core, Devon's protective instincts when it came to Rae knew no bounds. Their former pact—the one where she stayed safely out of reach and allowed him to do all the heavy lifting—was brutally enforced.

After Simon managed to stiffly pull himself from the car, she stood blindly by while Devon ripped off his belt and wound it around Simon's wrists, securing it with a speed and skill that would have made his teachers back at the Oratory proud. If Simon recognized the technique, he didn't say so. He simply watched his progress with a little smile, standing perfectly still and taking deliberate care not to accidently brush up against Devon's skin.

The second it was finished, they were on the move. While Devon might have been reluctant to touch at any cost, he was even more reluctant to allow Simon to walk freely in such proximity to both his fiancée and his friends. Instead, Devon grabbed him roughly by the arm, steering him as quickly as possible over the rough gravel and safely inside.

The second they passed over the threshold, a tiny shiver rippled down Rae's skin. She looked up in dismay at the wooden rafters, realizing the obvious for the first time. While Simon's powers may not work inside the room, both hers and Devon's wouldn't work either.

Devon seemed to acknowledge their predicament at the same time. His fingers clenched into momentary fists, twitching in that restless way they did when stripped of their heightened sensitivity.

Then, sensing Simon's eyes upon him, he took a deep breath and willed them smooth. "Stay there," he said under his breath, pacing to the far wall.

Since none of the friends knew exactly how long they would be staying at the house, and their plans for the boathouse stretched no further than a necessary garage, the place had become a sort of catch-all for all the accumulated rubbish they didn't want cluttering the house.

There were old tennis rackets, an ancient-looking record player, the entire contents of the kitchen—since none of them had the faintest idea how to cook—and piles upon piles of Molly's old fashion magazines. Although they were useless to her now that the clothes had 'gone out of season,' she was still unwilling to throw them away.

Most of the space, of course, was taken up by the five or six luxury sports cars parked neatly inside. Even in stillness they looked fast, like at the faintest touch they might go flying through the door, never to be seen again.

Taking care of said cars, performing useless, routine maintenance, had become a sort of therapy to each of the boys during their stay. But Devon didn't spare them a glance as he weaved his way through and returned a moment later, with a heavy metal chair and a rope.

What are you going to do? she asked telepathically, eying the chair with skepticism. *The man almost took down an entire agency, you don't think he can best a single chair?*

She waited, but Devon never looked up in reply. It was only then that she remembered he couldn't hear her as long as they were inside these walls.

"So..." Simon began tentatively. He had been waiting patiently next to Julian's car, his hands folded politely in front of him despite their ties. "Have the two of you been staying here long?"

Devon and Rae shared a quick look, but neither one of them answered. Instead, Devon simply sank to his knees and began tying the legs of the chair to each of the surrounding cars.

Simon didn't seem to mind. In fact, he seemed thrilled just to be out in the open air and talking to people again. Especially since one of those people happened to be his only daughter.

"A lot of horsepower for just two people. And that was a big house." He cocked his head curiously. "You visiting here with friends?"

Again, the two of them came up short. While Rae cowered silently against the wall, trying her best not to act as shell-shocked as she felt, Devon finished his work and came to stand directly in front of him.

"Sit down," he said quietly, gesturing to the chair.

The command was firm, but he seemed incredibly reluctant to meet Simon's eyes. Again, Simon smiled to himself as he took a seat, placing his legs against the metal so Devon would have an easier time of binding him there. Once or twice, during the awkward process, Simon opened his mouth to speak. Once or twice, Devon's shoulders stiffened defensively, and he held his tongue.

When he finally did speak, it wasn't to his captor. It was to his daughter.

"Rae..." he ignored the extra hard tug Devon gave to the rope, and fixed his eyes on the far wall where she was hovering near the door, "...I can't tell you how long I've waited for this day."

There was a hitch in her breathing, and Devon's fingers paused over the rope.

"I have to admit," Simon's eyes grew soft as he looked at her, "a part of me didn't think it was ever going to happen. I had given up hope, surrendered myself to the fact that I would never escape the darkness of that cell. That I would remain there until the day I died."

There was a haunted sort of emptiness to his voice that, despite having already been through an exorbitant amount of pain, neither of the younger generation could begin to understand. A sort of hollow resignation that could only come from endless years of looking at the same four walls.

"I...went to prison once." Rae was as surprised by any of the rest of them to hear herself speaking. But after such a painful admission, she felt the need to contribute.

Devon glanced swiftly over his shoulder, and Simon's face lit up in surprise.

"Really?"

Great, Rae. That's the FIRST thing you want to tell your long-lost father? 'Don't worry, Dad, we actually have a lot in common. I'm an ex-con, too.'

The two men stared at her expectantly, and her face flushed with embarrassment.

"It was only for, like, two days..."

Devon's face tightened in a painful grimace, and he finished quickly with the knots. As he took a step back, Simon offered him up a calm smile.

"My apologies, young man. I seem to have relieved you of both your jacket and your belt in a single evening. I'll have to find a way to replace them."

Devon took a careful step back, highly unaccustomed to carrying on any semblance of 'friendly conversation' with men he'd just strapped to a chair. "Don't...uh..." he cleared his throat quickly, "don't worry about it."

Simon smiled again before returning his eyes to Rae. She hadn't moved more than an inch since they'd set foot in the boathouse. And besides her unexpected prison admission, she stayed perfectly quiet. It was as if she was simply waiting for something. For something to happen that would turn back the hands of time to a moment when the world made sense. To a moment before she'd opened that door, and life as she knew it had crumbled into a million pieces.

But whether that future would ever have been possible...neither of them would ever know.

"Sweetheart," he said gently. Rae looked up in alarm, and Devon leveled the prisoner with a chilling glare. "You don't really have a plan here, do you?"

A wave of incapacitation swept through Rae from her head to her toes. Here she was, one of the most capable agents in the history of the Privy Council. One of the two most powerful people who had ever set foot on the planet...but staring into the eyes of her resurrected father, she was nothing but a six-year-old girl again. Wide-eyed and trembling. Unable to answer a simple question.

Fortunately, she had a fiancé who was more than up to the task.

It seemed that Devon had taken the term 'sweetheart' very personally, because when he swept back towards Simon there wasn't an ounce of that childhood-ingrained fear left on his face.

"The plan is to keep you alive, providing you don't make us regret doing it," he said savagely, spitting the words out through his teeth. "A line you're already flirting with."

"Devon," Rae said in soft reproach.

Simon, however, couldn't have been more riveted. He leaned forward, looking nothing short of delighted, peering eagerly at Devon in the dark.

"*Devon?*" he repeated in surprise. "*That's* who...of course, I should have known." His eyes twinkled as he leaned back against the chair. "Devon, you got all your teeth."

All the fierce threats and anger melted clean away as Devon froze in place, looking suddenly pale. He made a compulsive movement with his mouth, like he was checking with his tongue just to make sure, before taking a step back, looking incredibly disturbed. "Uh...yeah. Thanks?"

Simon chuckled, a surprisingly friendly sound no matter what kind of shadow his name cast. "When I first met you—you only had four. You were very proud of them," he remembered fondly. "Wouldn't stop showing me."

Devon's eyebrows lifted ever so slightly as his emotional limit for talking to living, breathing nightmares visibly overflowed. His body angled towards his fiancée, though he kept his eyes trained warily on her father. "...Rae?"

Like flipping a switch, Rae snapped back into action.

"Uh, yeah. Simon, you're going to stay here for the night. We'll be back in the morning with some food for you, and..." She paused, suddenly uncertain. "What do you like for breakfast?"

There was a slight pause during which Simon smiled at her affectionately, and Devon closed his eyes like he was ready to strangle her right there on the spot.

"He'll eat whatever we give him, Rae."

Her fiancé's voice was a note or two higher than usual, and his entire body was tilting towards the door—like he couldn't stand to be inside a moment longer.

"Right, of course." She nervously tucked her hair behind her ears, flushing with embarrassment. They had almost made it all the way out, when Simon called out softly once more.

"Rae?"

They paused in unison, and turned around. He gazed intently into her eyes.

"...do you think you're ever going to call me *Dad*?"

The door slammed shut.

Out in the open air, it was easier to think. For that matter, it was easier to worry. As the power of their ink coursed back into their bodies, Rae nervously glanced over her shoulder.

"Do you think we should have gagged him?"

It shouldn't technically be necessary. The boathouse was too far away from the manor for anyone besides Devon and her to hear what was going on. And the manor itself was too far away from any other house to pose the slightest bit of problem.

But still...you never knew.

Devon gave her another exasperated look before winding his arm around her waist and pulling her into his chest with a sigh. "I think we should have gagged you."

Chapter 4

Sure enough, the entire house was fast asleep by the time Rae and Devon finally made it in from the boathouse. Every light was still shining, but lately it was hardly an indication of anything, one way or another. Ever since waking up the morning after the fight—huddled together in the same tiny hospital room—the group's priorities had suddenly shifted.

A sense of security, normalcy, was prized above all else. To go back to a moment in time when the nightmares were held at bay, when they were able to close their eyes and breathe. It had become the unspoken obsession. A collective treatment to the darkness that had descended upon them like a fog. The whole reason for the house. The reason for the isolation. The single goal all of them were striving desperately to achieve.

The television had also been left on for good measure. Quiet, like the darkness, had become an unspoken taboo. One to be avoided at all costs.

Staged audience laughter followed Rae and Devon as they made their way through the living room and up the stairs. A black and white sitcom probably none of them had ever seen. Devon made a slight detour and turned it off before joining Rae at the base of the stairs.

"Do you think I should sleep on the couch?" he asked quietly.

She gazed at him questioningly, eyes flickering between him and the sofa. "Down here? Why would you—"

"In case anything happens." He glanced automatically at the front door, as if he could see through it to the boathouse just beyond. "I could get over there faster, if—"

"Nothing's going to happen," she assured him quickly. "You used more than sixty feet of rope, Dev; *I* couldn't get out of that chair. And even if we did hear something, we could jump out of the second-floor window just as quickly as the door."

"But if he—"

"*Hey,*" she placed a steadying hand on his arm, pulling him gently towards the stairwell, "it's going to be fine. We'll go out there first thing in the morning, I promise. Until then, come to bed."

He hesitated, unable to choose between her confidence and her safety.

"You know I can't heat the bed up by myself." Her voice fell to a low whisper as she stretched up on her toes and kissed his ear. "It's way too big for just one person."

The corners of his lips twitched up in a little smile, and he inclined his head so they were angled towards each other. She could feel his warm breath on her forehead; his fingers came down to trace the hollowed curve beneath her eyes.

"I love you, Rae Kerrigan," he murmured. "You know that, right? No matter who your father happens to be. No matter what kinds of crazy things you want to store in our boathouse."

They kissed swiftly, but sweetly. Her eyes closed in a contented smile. He had said the name right that time. 'Kerrigan.' He'd said it the way it was supposed to be.

"I love you, too." She kissed him once more before pulling back to tenderly stroke his face. Then, with no warning whatsoever, her eyes lit with mischief and she went simultaneously limp.

No one else in the world could have reacted in time, but Devon caught her without a moment's pause, scooping her up in his arms with a low chuckle.

"You want me to carry you over the threshold again?"

She wrapped her arms around his neck, and peered up at him with a little smile.

"Yes, please."

And so he did. Just like the night before. And the night before that.

Rae was sort of hoping to get a restful night's sleep, then wake up recharged with some brilliant new plan in the morning. Except she was sadly mistaken. She doubted she had gotten more than thirty minutes at a time. Each time she'd finally dozed off, she'd hear some imaginary creak, or rattle, or the sound of a coil of rope falling to the ground, and she'd bolt upright again. And again.

Apparently, she wasn't the only one.

Devon laid beside her only until she managed to close her eyes the first time. After that, he'd gotten soundlessly to his feet and perched upon the windowsill, gazing unblinkingly down at the makeshift jail. Rae was able to gauge what time it was by the shift in moonlight across his long, silvery hair. By the time it started to lighten to its usual brown, she threw off the covers and gave up on sleeping once and for all.

He glanced over his shoulder with a sympathetic smile. "Good morning."

"That's one way of putting it." She sat upright with a sigh, shoving her messy curls back out of her face. The streams of early sunlight mercilessly stung her eyes, and the silken straps of the lingerie nightgown Molly had bought her as an engagement present had twisted themselves into an elegant chokehold. She struggled with them petulantly for a moment, before giving up on that as well.

Devon chuckled and tore himself away from the window to join her on the bed. Whether it was his extra year being out in the field, or simply the fact that he had always been impossibly resilient, the night of sleepless worry seemed to have little effect on him. Besides a faint shadow beneath his eyes, Rae would never have known he spent the entire evening on lookout. And in this house, that shadow was hardly going to stand out amongst any of their friends.

"Here, let me help you with that." He eased her around and began unravelling the straps. One hand held her hair as the other worked with an easy grace. A second later, the knots that held her captive came undone.

A second after that...the entire slip fell off.

"Devon!" she gasped, clasping it securely against her chest.

There was a creak on the bed as he scooted surreptitiously closer.

"Oh...I'm sorry." His eyes widened with false innocence, gazing back at her without apology or shame. "I must have unlooped it somehow."

Despite the tension coursing through her body, Rae felt herself start to grin. These sorts of diversionary tactics had become par for the course, not only with them but with the entire house.

There was only so long you could live your life under a constant state of siege, before nerves began fraying, tempers started cracking, and the whole thing threatened to unravel. Instead, they sought levity and laughter wherever they could. Joking about Charlie and his crush on the way into the Privy Council. Ripping your fiancée's nightgown to initiate sex when there was a prisoner strapped to a chair just a stone's throw from the window. You know, just the usual stuff.

It was never the right time. But that was basically the point. When was the right time? When you lived under the threat of darkness for so long, you started forcing moments of light.

"I didn't want it to come to this," Devon muttered, shaking his head as he slipped off his pants and pulled his shirt over his head.

She giggled and tried to shimmy out from under him, but he pinned her arms above her head, lowering himself on top of her with an air of martyred resignation. His fingers eased the silk away from her tight clutches, and started trailing it down her ivory skin.

"But I guess since it's coming apart anyway, we could always—"

There was a knock on the door.

Both froze.

"Hey, you guys up?"

Devon practically fell off the bed as Rae hastened to cover herself with a pillow. Their eyes locked upon the handle, and for a moment Rae could practically hear both their hearts pounding guiltily as a thousand unspeakable *Kerrigan* scenarios flashed suddenly through their heads.

Have we been found out already?! Did something happen? But Devon was watching all night! He would've seen if anything went wrong!

There was another knock, gentler this time.

"Devon? Rae?"

As usual, Devon was the first to recover himself. "Yeah," there was barely a hint of annoyance in his voice, "what's up, Luke?" It was a testament to his skills as a covert operative that he was able to infuse even an ounce of normalcy into his speaking. Not enough to fool most people, but enough to get by in a pinch.

He and Rae exchanged a quick look, then they held their breath, waiting for a response.

A response that turned out to be as innocuous as any they could have hoped for.

"I'm heading to that market in town to get some breakfast. Molly had a bad night with the baby, and I need to pick up some more of those anti-nausea pills. You guys want anything?"

Rae let out a silent sigh of relief, while Devon ran his hands over his face. He resurfaced with a faint smile. "No, man. We're cool. Thanks."

"Alright. See you soon. Sorry if I woke you."

It wasn't until he was walking away, not until they heard his footsteps descending the stairs, that Rae and Devon realized the horrific implications of what he'd said. What a little trip into town might mean... when all the cars were housed in the garage.

"WAIT!"

They called out at the same time, blurring into action as they hastened to get dressed. Devon stumbled frantically to the door, yanking on a pair of jeans as he did so, while Rae sprang to her feet and conjured a thick trench coat, pulling it on over nothing but a pair of lacy panties. She was still knotting the belt when Devon ripped open the door and half-fell out into the hallway, taking just a second to get his bearings before sprinting to the stairs.

In a last-ditch effort, he decided just to jump instead, landing right in front of Luke as he was reaching for the front door.

"Hey," he ignored Luke's look of surprise and casually leaned against the doorknob, as if these sorts of dramatic entrances were an everyday occurrence, "actually, Rae and I were wanting to head into town anyway. Why don't you let us pick up breakfast today?"

As if on cue, Rae skidded to a stop at the top of the stairs, her boots making an angry screeching sound as she clutched desperately at the belt of her coat. Well aware that two sets of eyes were fixed upon her, she smoothed down her hair and made a conscious effort to descend the steps with as much dignity as she was able to muster.

In hindsight, it was a good thing they got Luke—not one of the others. While Molly and Julian read into every little detail, Luke was by far the most easy-going of the gang. Even if that quality had been pushed to the brink as of late, he was still able to let these little eccentricities roll off his shoulders in a way of which the others were incapable.

In hindsight, it also would've been alright if they got Angel. She simply didn't care.

"Okay." He raised his eyebrows but stepped back with a little grin, amused by the uncharacteristically feeble efforts being made by his friends. "Just be sure you get the bottle with the blue lettering. The other stuff didn't work. And she says she doesn't want fruit today. *Just* bagels."

Molly Skye? Trespassing into the forbidden world of carbs? She must have had a really bad night...

"Got it," Devon said quickly, still blocking the door.

The one thing that hadn't changed at all since the fight were his adorably over-the-top efforts to help as much as he could with Molly's turbulent pregnancy. From cherry ice cream runs to coconut bath oil, he'd gotten it all. Rae had even caught him browsing online for cribs with Julian, before she'd suggested gently that might be something that Molly and Luke wanted to do together.

"Cool, well...thanks." Luke headed back to his own bedroom, casting another quirky smile over his shoulder as he went. "Have fun with...whatever the hell is going on this morning."

Rae blushed and nodded as Devon gave him a mock salute. The second he was gone, however, the two of them turned to each other in mild panic.

"What the heck are we going to do now?" Rae asked quietly.

Devon held her gaze for a moment before his training kicked in and he assumed a practiced sort of calm, prioritizing their problems one at a time.

"I'm going to go out to the boathouse to make sure that Simon's ties held, and he didn't get up to any mischief in the middle of the night."

Rae nodded quickly, glancing nervously out the window towards where her biological father was bound in rope to her fiancé's favorite car. "Yeah, that's a good idea. We'll go do that."

She started marching automatically towards the door, but Devon caught her gently by the shoulders and turned her right back around. "No—*I'll* go do that. You, my dear, have your own mission to complete."

"My own mission...?"

Her face blanked, but he tucked her hair behind her ears with a little smile.

"You've got to get some bagels."

Bagels...right.

She considered it for a second before her mouth twisted up into a wry grin. "You sure gave me the more dangerous task, didn't you? All those bakeries... so little time..."

He chuckled and lifted his coat off the rack by the door, slipping it over his shoulders before giving her a quick kiss on the forehead. "Please, don't fight me on this. He poses a much smaller risk to me than he does to you. I don't...I don't even want to think about it."

She bowed her head, but didn't put up a word of resistance. Devon was allowing her to play out the scenario with her father. The least she could do was allow him the basic protections. "Okay," she kissed him again before grabbing the keys to the work car, "I'll be back soon as I can." She swept out the door without another word, unwilling to stay lest she change her mind and insist on going along with him. The brisk morning air bit into her face the second she walked outside, and she slipped into a tatù just to get to the car faster.

Devon might be right about a lot of things. Heck—he might be right about most things. But this, he was wrong about.

Simon Kerrigan didn't pose a *small* risk to anyone. Not by a longshot...

Thirty minutes later, Rae was speeding back to the house.

She'd made it to the market in record time. Hurried down the aisles, trying to ignore how surreally ordinary the whole thing felt. Found the anti-nausea pills with the blue lettering. Purchased a gigantic crate of bagels.

But no matter how fast she went, or how sweetly she smiled at the cashier just to get them to hurry along, she only had one thing on her mind.

Devon's with my father right now. Devon's with my father.

It looped there like an unholy chant, raising the hair on the back of her neck as she flew over the English countryside on her way home.

Home.

Funny, it was somehow easy to think of it that way. First New York had been home, then Guilder, then London. Then the farmhouse in Scotland.

And now...this secluded mansion in Kent.

Not one of them was any more authentic than the next. All of them had some legitimate claim. And yet, whenever Rae warmed to the notion of 'home,' she found that not a single one of them leapt to mind. Because when she pictured home, she didn't picture the place.

She pictured the people.

A short, but tender roster of faces scrolled quickly through her mind. Faces of the best people she knew. All of them, hiding in that lovely house.

And here, she had brought this new disaster right to their doorstep.

Her foot pressed down on the gas and the car shot forward, making it back to the mansion in record time. She swung into the nearest parking space and was out of the car before the engine had even cut out, marching frantically towards the entrance to the boathouse.

Devon was leaning against the front of it, staring towards the house, his eyes lost in thought. He glanced up quickly when she rounded the corner and flashed her a quick smile. "You got the bagels?"

She held up the bag, but focused entirely upon the door. "How did it go? Is everything alright? Is he still tied up in there? Maybe we should—"

"Hey," Devon stepped deliberately into her line of sight, calming her down, "just take a breath, okay? He's still in there. Everything's fine. Now that you're back, we just have to figure out what to do next." He tilted her head down and caught her eye. "Alright? Can you do that?"

She nodded hastily, but for the millionth time since she'd gotten up that morning she came up frustratingly blank. "You're right. You're absolutely right. But, Devon... I still don't know what we're supposed to do. Nothing has changed since yesterday. They're still going to murder him the second he's taken into custody before the trial—"

"But, babe, he *can't* stay here." Devon cast a glance behind him with a shudder, and Rae suddenly wondered as to what exactly had transpired in the boathouse that morning. "You said it yourself: it's a miracle that no one's already stumbled across him. No matter what happens next, we've got to get him out of here before someone else—"

"Hey, guys!"

It was a testament to how shaken up both Devon and Rae were that neither one of them had heard Julian walking over to them across the grass. They whirled around in alarm, but for once in his life their beloved psychic didn't seem to notice.

He had gotten dressed today, an occasion indeed. Moving briskly across the grass in dark jeans and a leather jacket. Dark hair pulled back into its customary ponytail, and a rather unexpected smile lighting up his face.

It's because he finally got some sleep last night, Rae thought to herself, looking him over. *I only heard him scream one time.*

The battle at the factory had been particularly hard on their clairvoyant friend. Still reeling from the attempted murder of his girlfriend just a few days before, Julian had been extra vigilant when it came to protecting Angel from the worst of the fighting. Of course, Angel was never really one to shirk a fight. As such...they had found themselves in a bit of a tight spot.

When Devon, Gabriel, Kraigan, and Rae had all disappeared to go after Cromfield, the battlefield was suddenly missing some key players. As a result, their opposition was left with a suddenly small list of high-value targets. And between his skill as a warrior and his innate ability to see the future, Julian had been top of that list.

Despite suffering devastating casualties in the process, they had forced him and Angel onto a rickety steel bridge with enemies advancing on them from both sides. The two lovers fought back to back, inflicting unspeakable devastation, but still they were still outnumbered fifty to one.

In the end... it had been a matter of fate.

There had come a moment amidst all the bloodshed and fighting, where Julian's eyes had flashed suddenly white. His body had frozen in place, and when he shook himself back to the present he was a different man.

His hand had reached behind him and grabbed Angel. She turned, and for a split second the entire world had seemed to stop.

"Do you trust me?" he breathed.

Her sapphire eyes widened but she nodded her head, flinching back as a bullet ripped through the air just inches from the side of her face.

"I trust you."

The air around them started to shimmer, and a single tear fell down his face. Then, without stopping to think, he took her in his arms and threw them both over the side of the bridge.

They fell through a pane of glass, and hit the ground just as the entire thing exploded.

The vision Julian had seen gave him the chance to save everyone. Over a hundred people, although every single one of them wanted to see him dead.

He chose to save only himself and Angel instead.

It was the right thing to do.

Rae, Devon, Luke, and Molly had told him a million times over. Beth had told him. Fodder had told him. Even Gabriel had broken his self-imposed isolation long enough to send him a text.

None of it mattered.

Behind those beautiful eyes, Julian still saw every one of their faces. As clearly as if he was still trapped up on that bridge, knowing that every single one of them was going to die.

The screaming last night made sense. The smile this morning didn't.

"What're you doing out here?" he asked curiously, gesturing to the bag. "Luke said that you guys were going to get breakfast?"

"Yeah," Rae recovered quickly, lifting the bag of bagels in the air, "you want one?"

He flashed her a quick smile, but shook his head. "Actually, I was thinking I was going to go out for a drive. Clear my head a little."

Both Rae and Devon froze in a moment of shared panic, torn completely in two.

They had been tirelessly encouraging Julian to get out of the house. Take in the fresh air. Do exactly what it was he'd just suggested. They should be thrilled.

Except, Julian's car was parked inside. In fact, it was currently anchoring the chair of a certain homicidal villain they'd recently kidnapped.

Fortunately, Devon had the perfect solution.

"Take my car," he said immediately, fishing around in his pocket for the keys.

Julian glanced up in surprise. The luxury sports car Devon had been gifted by the Crown Prince of England had been officially off-limits since Julian had accidently stalled it on the top of a hill in Scotland. Apparently, in the world of men that sort of thing was damn near unforgivable.

"Are you sure?" Julian caught the keys, looking a little confused. "We haven't even looked at the engine since that time. I don't want to accidentally break anything—"

"Nonsense." Devon flashed him an easy smile as he cut him off. "It's good you're going. You should enjoy the ride." He winked. "In a proper car."

Julian smiled tentatively, a sudden thrill of excitement dancing in his eyes as he looked down at the precious keys. "Thanks, man. That's really cool of you."

With a parting wave, he headed over to the boathouse.

Wait...NO!

Both Devon and Rae were quick to jump in his path.

"What're you doing?" Devon demanded, trying not to sound as agitated as he was. It was an act at which he failed spectacularly.

Julian paused, looking curiously him up and down.

"I'm...getting the car?"

Devon shook his head quickly, trying his best to coax his friend the other way. "The car's parked around behind the house, remember? By that old tool shed."

An unintentional tremor shook his voice, and Julian frowned.

"No. You moved it inside after it started to rain."

He took another step forward, but before his foot even hit the ground Devon snatched the keys right back out of his hands. "Actually, I don't want you driving my car after all. You'll only mess it up again."

Rae's eyes snapped shut in a grimace. *Nice, Devon. Real smooth.*

Julian raised his eyebrows, but let it go.

"Fine. Whatever. No need to be a dick." He pulled his own keys out of his pocket instead and started heading for the garage, but before he'd taken more than two steps—Devon had snatched those away as well.

Oh crap. This is going to end badly.

Sure enough, Julian's unexpectedly good mood faded completely away as he took a step backwards, glaring at his best friend. "What the hell are you doing?"

Devon simply froze.

From the day Rae had first met him, Devon Wardell could lie better than anyone she'd ever seen. It wasn't that he was inherently duplicitous, quite the contrary. He just had an innate ability to twist the moment's narrative to whatever would best help his cause.

She had seen him talk down ambassadors and diplomats. She'd seen him steal information from corporate executives, only to sell it back to them after being hired for its recovery. She'd once seen him convince an entire mob of people that he couldn't be the man they were looking for, because he'd grown up on a simple farm in Eastern Ukraine.

Needless to say, when it came to storytelling Devon was a champion.

...but none of that mattered when it came to Julian.

Bromance was understating it. Best friends was understating it. The two of them were closer than brothers. Close to a point where they were fundamentally incapable of keeping even the most trivial details from each other. There's probably never been a partnership in the Privy Council as close as these two. Or a friendship.

They tagged along to each other's haircuts. Had long, whiskey-filled conversations trying to interpret each other's dreams. Devon had even confessed that, in the high of completing a mission, they had once contemplated getting matching tattoos.

It simply wasn't in their nature to lie. Not to each other.

And right on cue, Devon started to unravel.

"Don't...don't go out for a drive." In a fit of nervous energy, he started tossing the keys back and forth so fast they became nothing but a silver blur. "The roads are really icy, and—"

"Dev," Julian interrupted, shaking his head, "what are you—"

"I'm pretty sure the Jag is out of gas anyway. So there's no point in trying to—"

"No, it isn't. I just filled it up. What the hell is going—"

"I was hoping we could have breakfast together!"

Not his strongest line, but unfortunately that was the one Devon chose to end on.

This time, Julian turned to Rae as if hoping she'd offer up some simple explanation for her fiancé's behavior. Something like, he's been chewing on paint chips. He's *really* drunk. Something that might make it make sense. When she dropped her eyes to the ground, he turned back to Devon.

"What's going on?" he asked her.

There was no leniency in his voice now. No humor. No anger. Just a chilling straightforward desire to get to the truth. One that would be satisfied at all costs.

She wasn't sure how to respond, and glanced at Devon.

He also heard the shift in Julian's tone, and his face paled. He shot Rae a desperate look as well before staring down at his shoes. "We got bagels..."

On any other day, Julian would have simply seen for himself. He would have tranced out where he stood, and looked ahead to the future to unlock the secrets of their past. There was a reason that no one in the group could hide anything from him. Whether they liked it or not, he was the closest thing to omniscient the gang had.

But Julian didn't do that. He didn't use his tatù. His eyes stayed dilated and dark.

Instead, he simply pushed past Devon and threw open the door to the boathouse.

"Jules, no—"

But it was too late.

Together, Rae and Devon watched as he swept inside, blinking several times as his eyes adjusted to the sudden darkness. He gasped when he saw the man with the beard.

"Hello," Simon smiled cheerfully. "And who might you be?"

Julian's mouth fell open and he took a step back.

"Guys...what the hell did you do?"

Chapter 5

Rae could have heard a pin drop.

And not just because of her tatù.

Four pairs of eyes shot in opposite directions. Then, with no further preamble, Rae and Devon started speed-talking at the same time. As hard as they'd tried to keep their secret, they were suddenly unable to hold it in for even a second longer.

"We found him in one of the cells down in the old factory."

"Ford was going to shoot him right there on the spot."

"Couldn't just leave him. The place has public access."

"Right there on the spot, Jules. No trial. No witnesses."

"I told her it was a bad idea to take him here, but we couldn't think of any—"

"I couldn't just let them shoot him in the head!"

Both voices had risen in panic the more they rambled, so that by the time Rae's screeching wail ended the conversation she was panting with guilt and fear. So was Devon. It wasn't until she looked up and saw Julian's blank expression that she realized he had no idea what they were talking about.

"I'm sorry..." Julian held up a tentative hand, trying to slow down the frantic pace of the confession, "...Who is this guy?"

Words failed Rae. Devon, too. Apologies failed them. Desperate, Rae and Devon ended up turning to Simon, who returned their silent panic with a low chuckle. Then, with that same smile warming his haggard face, he turned his eyes to Julian. A smile that looked pleased, and oddly somewhat sad. "Decker, right? You've got to be related to Jacob Decker."

Julian took half a step forward, lost in confusion. "I'm his son."

This time, it was Simon who sucked in a sharp breath. Whatever he'd been expecting Julian to say, it certainly wasn't that. As he looked him up and down once more, a strange expression came over his face. One that looked almost repentant. Which turned into one that looked almost relieved.

A second later, it was replaced with that disconcerting smile that was starting to annoy Rae.

"Simon Kerrigan. Nice to meet you. Again. Been a long time."

Why the hell couldn't the cell just have been empty...

Julian took a small step back, then a much larger one. Then he backed all the way up to the open door. He didn't seem to know where to look, or even how to look. His pupils were wide and fixed, but his lips turned up into a reflexive, disbelieving kind of smile. He laughed once. Short and humorless. Then began to lose himself in the echoing silence that followed.

"No...no, he isn't." His eyes flashed up to Simon, as if the man was playing a cruel joke. "You're *not*—don't even say that. Devon, what is..." He turned to his friend for answers, but for one of the first times ever Devon came up blank.

"I'm sorry, Jules." His voice was as quiet as a grave. "I'm so sorry we didn't tell you. Rae and I only brought him here last night, and we didn't know how best to... We didn't want to involve the rest of you until we knew—"

"You didn't want to *involve* us?" Julian repeated incredulously.

It was impossible to tell whether he believed it was Simon. In fact, if Rae had to bet, she'd guess not. He clearly thought they both were crazy—that much was certain. From the way his fists kept clenching in belated panic, he probably thought they'd kidnapped a homeless man.

"Why is...I mean...what did you..."

Again and again, he tried to speak. Apparently was trying to understand. Again and again, he came up blank. The edges of his eyes began clouding white but he contained it, like a winter storm that never got off the ground. Finally he simply turned back to Simon, at a compete loss. "Is that your belt, Dev?"

Devon's eyes darted to the bindings on Simon's wrists, and he flushed before marching forward to retrieve it. "Yeah, I... We were in a bit of a hurry."

"Jules?" Rae tentatively rested her hand on his shoulder, purposely ignoring the way he jumped at her touch.

If there was anyone in the house who was vital to get on board, any one person whose compliance could persuade the rest of them—it was Julian. His opinion and approval carried a weight to it that surpassed even her own. There was a steadiness about him that people trusted. A wisdom that went even beyond his ability to see things that were yet to come.

But this? Clearly Julian was not willing to get on board with it.

"What makes you think he's your father?" he asked quietly. It was the first direct question he'd been able to manage, and Rae answered it very seriously.

"I recognize him from pictures, and from... from the time I went back to see the past." She lowered her voice defensively, aware that Simon was still very much able to hear her. "And then, when we found him at the factory, one of the older guards with us recognized him as well. Somehow, he didn't die in the fire, Jules. Cromfield saved him. Stashed him away all these years as his prisoner." *And never told me. Freakin' Cromfield wanted to tell me everything else, but just happened to forget to mention this one thing?*

The prophetic white started swirling around in his eyes once more, and he took a deep breath to get it under control.

"I know you'd probably like to believe that." His voice gentled a fraction of an inch. "No one wants their father to be dead, no matter how much he..." His voice cut off guiltily, and Simon flashed him a sympathetic smile.

"No matter how much he deserved it?" Simon finished knowingly. Julian flushed and Simon smiled once more, bowing his head to his chest. "Yes, I deserved to be in that prison. The things I did, the people I hurt—not the least of whom are standing in this room... It was unforgivable." His eyes rested briefly on Rae before he continued on quietly, "But things have changed. *I've* changed. I had to. Spend enough time in the darkness, it'll change anyone. Even someone like me. I'm not lost to it anymore. Of that I can assure you."

A ringing silence fell on this proclamation. One during which each of the friends stared back with matching distrust.

Simon chuckled again and cocked his head to the side. "Not the answer you were hoping for?"

Julian stifled a shudder.

"I was hoping you came with the boathouse..."

Devon took a step forward, angling himself subconsciously in between. "Jules, we—"

"What's the plan here?" Julian interrupted. He seemed willing to allow Rae a secret or two on occasion. Even about something as great as this. That leniency did not apply to Devon.

Rae glanced between them then shook her head, deciding to come clean. "I honestly don't know. The guards back at the factory were willing to shoot him on the spot. I'm afraid that if we take him in, it's going to be the exact same thing. He'll never make it through the front door."

If Julian was at all surprised that she'd care one way or another, he didn't let on. He simply nodded silently and waited for her to continue.

"It was late, everyone was armed... I... I guess I panicked. I swore them all to secrecy and decided to stash him here until I could come up with a better plan."

Julian stared at her for a moment before returning his gaze to Simon. A better plan than this? The longer he stood there, the more ludicrous her hasty stop-gap solution seemed to be.

The ropes branched out from the chair like a giant spider web. Twisting and knotting in a geometric arch with Simon sitting right there in the middle. Devon's coat was on the floor behind him, and his belt was still hanging loosely from Simon's hands.

If there was to be a *better plan*, this certainly wasn't it.

"Well, he can't stay in here," Julian finally said, striding forward. "It dipped below freezing last night. You keep him out here too long, he'll get hypothermia and die."

Again, if he saw that as a particularly bad thing, he didn't let on. He simply knelt to the floor in front of the chair, and slowly started untying Devon's knots.

Rae and Devon exchanged a swift look, but neither one moved an inch. It was for the best that they had someone here with a fresh perspective. Someone whose reasoning centers hadn't been blunted by the trauma of that cave. But that still didn't mean he was entirely on board.

"Jules," Devon cleared his throat softly and knelt as well. He was still absentmindedly holding the keys he'd confiscated earlier, and they jingled quietly in his hand. "If there's anything he needs, we can bring it out here. I just don't feel comfortable with—"

"There's no bathroom. No lighting. No food or water. He's too far away for most of us to hear if something goes wrong, and the tips of his fingers are already turning blue." Julian's eyes skipped sharply over Devon, and landed upon Rae. "You want to save him, right? You want to keep him alive?" She bit her lip and nodded, refusing to meet her father's eyes. Julian turned back to the chair and continued working. "Then he comes inside."

Devon didn't say a word and stood back up, watching with silent, worried eyes as, one by one, the ropes began to fall. Every time Julian leaned within reach of Simon's hands, Devon's muscles tensed as if to throw himself in between.

But nothing happened.

Simon was the model prisoner. Sitting both quietly and patiently as the youngsters had briefly talked the problem through. Contributing not a single opinion.

When Julian undid the buckle and removed Devon's belt, he actually said a quiet word of thanks.

He received no reply.

"And what about the rest of them?" Rae asked softly as her father got stiffly to his feet. It didn't matter whether she could use ink in the room or not. Her hands were ready no matter what. "What about Molly?"

"Molly's tough," Julian fired back sharply, getting to his feet as well. "And the rest of them have a right to know what's going on inside their own house."

The unspoken accusation cut through the air, but it required no response. It was already in the past. Simon was loose now. There was no time to dwell.

But again...Devon proved the exception to this rule.

"Jules, I'm really sorry," he said under his breath as Simon stretched out his atrophied legs and began limping slowly to the door. "I should have told you."

Julian straightened up with a shrug. "I should have seen it coming." He dropped the rest of the rope to the floor, and carelessly tossed the chair Simon had been sitting in to the side. Carelessly, or strategically? It sailed through the air before coming down straight upon Devon's prized car—shattering the windshield into a million, glassy pieces.

Devon sucked in a gasp, hand to his chest as if he could literally feel the car's pain.

But Julian merely clapped him on the shoulder with a righteous smile. "You should have seen that coming, too."

The walk back to the house seemed endless. Even more so when the trio had to move along at Simon's shuffling, malnourished pace.

A part of Rae took in her father's tremoring hands and the sallow tint to his skin with a distant kind of concern. Should she be calling a doctor? Would Alicia make house calls this far away from London? More importantly, would Alicia consent to treat such a man even if she did?

But another part was far more focused on the immediate happenings than on any long-term treatment for the man who was supposed to have been her father. She kept her eyes trained on the house, thinking of the three people inside it. Wondering how each of them would react.

She wanted to just ask Julian. He had unlocked her future's secrets for so long, she was rather unaccustomed to waiting. But it wouldn't do any good. If he hadn't tranced out to see what was coming in the boathouse, then he wasn't going to do it right now. Especially as they were all about to find out.

One way or another...

Molly was downright impossible to guess. Her behavior was erratic enough even without an onslaught of hormones racing through her system, not to mention the fact that they were literally talking about Simon Kerrigan. In all likelihood, her reaction would be based one hundred percent upon however Rae felt. While Devon was protective above all else, Molly was empathetic. Even if Rae's judgement was temporarily misguided, her best friend would fight to see it through.

That just left Luke and Angel.

Luke was going to have his unique Knights' perspective. Rae wasn't sure if that was actually a good or a bad thing. And Angel...?

Her mind swam as she considered Angel.

If Cromfield had taken her father prisoner, that had to mean that Simon had somehow gotten himself onto the man's radar. In a way, it was hardly surprising—seeing as they were doing pretty much the same thing, at the same time, in the same city. In fact, it wouldn't be too much of a stretch to think that they had crossed paths at some point. Collaborated? Compared notes?

The fact that Simon had been kept alive said wonders. None of the rest of Cromfield's prisoners had made it. The other cells Rae had opened had been either empty, or scattered with bones. Simon's survival implied a personal connection of some sort.

Either way, Angel wouldn't have been old enough to remember. She would have been just a baby at the time that Simon was still free and walking the streets.

Rae's breath caught at the sudden realization. *What about Gabriel?*

Rae sighed quietly, and pushed her long hair out of her eyes. What *about* Gabriel? She'd been asking herself that same question for over a week.

After Carter's funeral, the guy was a ghost. Everyone knew where he was, of course. Locked away in that dingy, unfurnished apartment with enough booze to satisfy an entire army. But just knowing where he was didn't make him any more accessible. It didn't make him any less distant.

Rae's mind flashed back, and she remembered the day with perfect, terrible clarity. It had been raining. Ironically, that was the only thing that managed to cheer her up. Good. It should be raining. A silent tribute that the world itself knew what it had lost. Carter deserved that. The flowers were set, the eulogy read, and she had stood by her mother's side and watched as they lowered the casket into the ground.

In all her days... she had never seen anything more terrible.

Miserable didn't begin to cover it. The place was *gutted*.

People had come from far and wide. Flying in from cities in countries Rae had never even heard of. Carter had touched that many people. In no way was she surprised.

But by far, the hardest faces to see were the ones standing next to her.

Her mother was a wreck. A wreck, in that she didn't seem like a wreck at all. She simply stood there, never moving, never talking. Her blue eyes never leaving the coffin. It was as if her grief transcended any kind of ritual or understanding. She was on a different level altogether. Cold, and collected, and very much alone.

Not so contained were the rest of Rae's friends.

Molly had openly wept during the entire service, pressing her face into Luke's jacket as her body shook with silent sobs. Julian kept a hand on her shoulder, but it was as much to hold himself up as it was to comfort. He, too, was silently crying. Staring at the coffin in muted disbelief as a river of tears poured down his face.

Devon didn't actually cry, but in a way he looked even more devastated. He and Carter had shared a special bond. An unspoken closeness and accountability that had grown deeper with each passing year. There was a reason Carter had chosen Devon to be his best man—he thought of him as a son. And it was no secret that Devon had always looked to Carter as a substitute father. His hand had been clenched into a tight fist during the entire ceremony. It wasn't until after it was finished that Rae realized he had been holding the watch Carter had given him upon his graduation from Guilder. He'd left the watch on the coffin.

Rae watched the proceedings like a person trapped in a dream. It was as if the entire world had turned upside-down. Nothing felt real. The colors were too dim, then too bright. The flowers seemed to wilt the longer she stared. The sound of children's laughter drifted down from a playground four blocks up the street. But that couldn't be right. How could anyone be laughing today? How could anyone manage to laugh ever again?

It was the last time she saw her stepfather. It was also the last time she saw Gabriel.

He had been standing directly across from her, on the other side of the coffin. During the entire, hour-long service he'd never looked up a single time.

Rae remembered it in excruciating detail. The moment of her mentor's death. The way he'd burst into the room without any of them realizing it—unwilling to let the children he loved so much take the entire risk upon themselves. The way he'd jumped without thinking right in front of Gabriel as the bullet was fired. Absorbing it into his own chest instead. The way he'd died before he even hit the floor, leaving shell-shocked Gabriel standing in his wake.

From the look on his face, Rae guessed that he was remembering it as well. Playing it again and again through his mind. Trapped in a nightmarish loop. One that he couldn't get out of. One that he didn't want to get out of. One that had claimed him—body and soul.

After the funeral was over, he had just... gone.

Rae's face tightened as she stared down at the grass, brought back to the present. Simon was moving slowly a few paces back, and Julian had quickly hopped on the bandwagon of 'he doesn't get near enough to Rae to touch her.' Both men were flanking him on either side, leaving her in momentary solitude.

For a moment, she thought about calling Gabriel. She had vowed to give the guy his space, but she was beyond worried about him and this would have been a perfect excuse. But the more she thought about it, the more she realized there wasn't any point.

If Gabriel had ever met Simon, surely he would have told Rae about it by now.

When the group got to the front door, they paused. Julian shifted up to the front with Rae, while Devon lingered back with Simon. Together, they pushed open the door.

"Hello?" Rae called tentatively, peering around the empty house. "Is anybody up?"

She felt like a kid knocking on the door on Halloween. Armed with the worst trick of all.

The walls rang with silence, not a person in sight. Julian stepped inside with a slight frown, peering around the empty living room and kitchen.

"They were all here when I went outside," he murmured. Over the years, the group had learned to be wary of unexplained disappearances. "I don't—"

But that's when they heard them. Or rather, that's when they were heard themselves.

"Rae?! Is that you?!"

Luke had never sounded more distressed. There was the sound of running water, followed by the shatter of a distant crash. "Guys—get up here!"

They didn't need to be told twice.

Without a moment's pause Rae and Julian took off sprinting up the stairs, leaping them three at a time. Devon followed at once, before remembering Simon. He glanced back at him with a fractured expression, then, throwing caution to the wind, grabbed his arm and pulled him along.

Molly was on the floor of the bathroom when they burst in. Prone and unresponsive.

"MOLLS?!"

Rae fell to her knees beside Luke, avoiding the shards of a broken mug which had been swept accidentally off the counter. She reached out automatically to lift her friend to a sitting position, but it quickly became clear that Molly wasn't going anywhere.

"What happened?!" she exclaimed, lowering herself to the floor as well and slipping a towel beneath Molly's cheek.

Up close, she looked even worse. There wasn't an ounce of color to her already pale skin, and despite the fact that she looked too exhausted to even open her eyes, her little body wouldn't stop trembling.

Luke was almost as pale. "She can't stop throwing up. All night she'd been at it, hours and hours. But it tapered off this morning and I thought she was through the worst of it. Then it came back with no warning and she can't seem to stop."

As if on cue, Molly's body lurched forward and she shot up to the toilet. Both Rae and Luke held back her crimson hair as she gasped for breath, her fingers clinging to the edge of the bowl.

"Oh, Molls..." Rae stroked her back in soothing circles, trying desperately not to act as frantic as she felt. To say that Molly's pregnancy hadn't been an easy one would be understating it to a massive degree. And she was only in her eighth week. "Just breathe, sweetie. Just breathe."

"I've seen morning sickness before, but this doesn't look like morning sickness." Luke blue eyes tightened helplessly as her body rocked forward again. "What if it's that other thing? Hyperemesis something or other? Should we take her to the hospital?"

Rae glanced back at Julian but he simply shook his head, looking almost as distraught as Luke. "I would if I could, but there are no decisions being made. It wouldn't help."

Rae nodded quickly and turned back to her friend, dabbing her face with a dampened washcloth. "Molly, honey, I'm going to call Alicia, okay? She'll know what to—"

"Alicia's still back in Scotland," Luke countered softly, "helping everyone still recovering from the fight. All the other tatùed doctors I know are over there as well. I want to take her to a regular hospital, but I don't know if something would look...unnatural." His hands slid manically back through his hair, and he looked on the verge of tears. "I just don't know what to do."

A throat cleared softly behind him, and he turned with the rest of the group to look at Simon for the first time. It had been almost easy to forget that he was even there, what with the prospect of something going wrong with Molly, but he made himself known now.

"I don't mean to overstep, but I don't think a hospital will be necessary. She's just caught in the convulsions now. If she can—"

He took a step forward, and Devon threw him into the wall. Not against the wall. Into it.

Luke's eyes widened in shock—probably more so at the sudden sight of a bearded man than with the fact that Devon had used him to break the house—and even Molly tried to lift her head off the porcelain to see what was going on.

Simon kept his eyes locked on Devon.

It had to have been strange, Rae realized as she watched them. To find oneself in such a reversal of position. Simon Kerrigan had taken down more people in his day than half the people on the Privy Council's most wanted list combined. By all accounts, he wasn't the kind of person who would take a threat lightly. By all accounts...he wouldn't take it at all.

Yet, there he was. Standing calmly amidst the crumbling plaster. Eyes glistening slightly as Devon's arm pressed against his throat.

"Don't," Devon growled between his teeth. "You don't go near her."

Whether he was talking about Rae or Molly, no one knew. Realistically, it was probably both.

Simon slowly lifted his arms, putting up not an ounce of resistance. "I can help." His eyes bypassed Devon and locked onto Rae, staring with soft sincerity deep into her eyes. "I can help."

For a moment, all was quiet. Then, standing unnoticed in the corner, Julian's eyes went white. He gazed into the future for a moment before blinking back to the present. Rae was the only one who'd watched him, and gave her an almost imperceptible nod.

A nod she returned to Simon.

The arm came down and Simon peeled himself off the wall. He flashed Rae a tentative smile as he walked past her, but just as he was about to kneel her eyes shot up in warning.

"Try anything..." She let the rest of it hang. He could imagine the worst.

For the second time, he locked eyes with her and nodded slowly. Then, with hands more delicate than one could imagine, he propped Molly carefully up against the wall.

"Re-wet that washcloth," he instructed softly, holding out his hand to Luke. Luke flashed Rae a look of bewilderment, but hurried to do as he was told. The next second, Simon was pressing it gently against the back of Molly's neck. "Hey, sweetie—it's Molly, isn't it?"

Sweetie?!

Rae flashed Devon a look but he simply shook his head, keeping his eyes trained on Simon and his hands at the ready.

Molly opened her bleary eyes and struggled to focus.

"Yeah...who're you?"

Simon simply smiled. "Molly, have you ever had the hiccups before?"

She nodded weakly as he dabbed at the sides of her neck.

"When you throw up this long, it's kind of like the hiccups. Even though the thing that triggered it has long since passed, your diaphragm keeps contracting anyway. You get caught in a kind of loop. All we need to do is get you steady enough to break that cycle."

As the rest of the kids froze, spellbound, he turned back to Luke. "Do you by chance have any ginger tea? Preferably with some raspberry?"

Luke turned automatically to Rae, holding out his hand.

"Rae?"

Without thinking Rae waved her fingers above her palm, conjuring a steaming mug.

Simon stared for a second, his eyes widening ever so slightly, before he took it and held it to Molly's face.

"Don't drink," he instructed quietly, "just sniff it. Inhale it slowly."

She did as she was told, breathing in the herbal steam as it flushed her clammy face. This went on for about a minute. Then the shaking slowed and finally stopped. A minute after that, she took the mug from Simon's hands and lifted it tentatively to her lips. "How did...how did you know how to do that?" she asked, taking a tiny sip.

His smile remained, though his face grew abruptly sad. "When my wife was pregnant, she had the same thing. I used to sit with her for hours on the bathroom floor. Ginger tea was the only thing that worked." His eyes locked on Rae for the briefest of moments, then they both looked away.

"Thank you." Luke flashed him a grateful smile, stroking Molly's damp hair away from her face. "Really. Thank you so much."

"Yes, thank you." Molly was sitting up on her own now, looking like hell warmed over, but smiling for the first time. The smile faded slightly as she gathered enough of her wits to wonder why she'd been rescued by what looked like Grizzly Adams. "But... I'm sorry... Who are you?"

This time, Simon seemed to rethink just announcing his name. Instead he leaned back on his heels, apparently tossing the ball in his daughter's court.

Rae braced herself against the shower with a little sigh. "Actually, we have something to tell all of you..."

Chapter 6

It was a testament to how grateful Molly and Luke were for Simon's help that his formal introduction wasn't met with instant screaming.

That came a minute later.

It was a testament to how bad Molly was still feeling that it didn't last very long.

As the boys took Simon downstairs to wait in the living room, Rae tucked her best friend back into bed. She was still incredibly weak from the events of the morning, and despite having just met a supposed dead man she didn't offer one word of protest.

"There you go," Rae said gently, helping her into bed. "Easy does it." She pulled the blankets up to Molly's chin, and tucked another pillow behind her head for good measure. "You think you're going to be able to get any sleep?"

Molly grinned faintly, her red-rimmed eyes standing in stark contrast to the paleness of her face. "I don't think I have much of a choice."

"That's the spirit."

But as Rae gave her hand a final squeeze and headed to the door, Molly called out weakly once more. "Rae... Are you happy? That he's alive?"

Rae hesitated, trying to consider the question as objectively as she could.

On the one hand, what kind of sicko would be upset to learn that their father, who everyone had assumed burned up in a fire, was alive and well? What kind of daughter wouldn't have at least some small part of her thrill with the opportunity to get to know her biological father? The man who should have raised her. The man who gave her his name.

On the other hand, what person in their right mind could be happy to see Simon Kerrigan?

In the end she merely offered Molly a forced smile, her fingers gripping tightly around the edges of the door. "I don't see that I have much of a choice." With that, she flipped off the light and gently closed the door behind her. Molly was asleep by the time she made it back to the stairs.

The men weren't in the living room, as Rae had thought they would be. Instead, they were positioned in a strategic circle around Simon in the kitchen. Apparently, one of them had taken note that the man hadn't eaten in two or three days. That was being remedied now. Rae assumed Julian had something to do with that.

"Rae," Simon looked up cheerfully as she walked into the room, "how's she feeling? Doing a little bit better?" He was seated at the table with a plate of biscuits and honey in front of him. On the edge of the placemat, a cup of fresh-brewed coffee was steaming into the air.

Rae resisted the urge to smile. Paper plate. Plastic knife. Styrofoam cup. That had all been Devon's doing. The honey was most likely Luke's.

"Yeah," she tucked her hair behind her ears, and leaned against the wall next to Julian, "she's doing a lot better. Thank you... Simon."

His lips twitched up with a slight smile. "You know, your mother always used to do that when she was nervous." When she blanked, he gestured to her hair. "Tucking it behind her ears. She did that on the first day I ever met her. Done it every day since."

"I think it's probably best if you refrain from talking about Beth while you're in this house," Devon advised coolly. "Things are strained enough as it is."

Simon's eyebrows lifted slightly when Devon used her first name, but he quickly returned to his coffee. "You're quite right. My apologies. At any rate, I'm sure I'll be seeing her soon enough."

The little group froze, casting nervous glances around their circle.

Simon paused, looking about with a slight smile. "She is still my *wife*, you know. No matter the circumstances of our parting, I would have assumed she'd still be one of your first calls."

Luke folded his arms tightly across his chest, diverting as best he could. "I think you're going to have enough problems as it is, Simon, without trying to reconcile with your wife."

He was grateful for the help, sure. But one cup of ginger tea didn't atone for the countless lives Simon had ruined during his heyday in London. The countless lives he had taken. The Knights were as keenly aware of his transgressions as the Council was. In some ways, even more.

"You look incredibly familiar..." Simon squinted slightly as he tried to place the face in his memory. Tried to age it up by a few dozen years. "You're Patrick Fodder's son, aren't you?"

Luke hesitated, but didn't seem the harm. He'd find out soon enough anyway.

"His grandson."

"Of course, of course." Simon smiled warmly. "You're far too young to have been anything else. That would mean that his son...? Anthony...?"

Luke nodded swiftly, eager to turn the conversational spotlight away from himself. "He has two sons. I'm the younger."

"And did you receive a tatù?"

The question fired out at a speed that startled all of them. Simon included. It was spoken as a reflex. An instinctual, supernatural hunger that couldn't be undone.

Rae stared at him warily as he slowly lowered his cup to the table.

"I'm sorry," he began to apologize, "I didn't mean to—"

"Try to eat, Mr. Kerrigan," Julian advised, providing a gracious end to the conversation, one way or another. "You're going to need your strength."

It was absolutely surreal. To hear him addressing Simon in such a normalized manner. *Mr.* Kerrigan. As if he could have been *Mr.* Fodder, or the father of any of them.

And speaking of...

From the second Julian opened his mouth, Simon was fixated on him once more. There was a reason the psychic usually hung back in the shadows, but in such close quarters it seemed that no one could escape the man's probing gaze.

"I'm sorry, I don't mean to make you uncomfortable." Simon's eyes twinkled as they studied Julian's face with an intensity that made the poor guy squirm. "I just can't get over it. You look *so much* like your father. It's almost like stepping back in time."

Julian fidgeted nervously, and tried to avoid his gaze.

"Tell me, has your gift progressed even further than his? Jacob Decker was already one of the most talented psychics the world had ever seen. If you have somehow managed to..." He trailed off suddenly, looking at Devon instead. His lips parted in momentary surprise, turning up into a beaming smile. "That's exactly the look Tristan always got before he decided he'd had enough of my rantings and punched me in the jaw."

The room went dead quiet, stiff with a sudden chill that Rae didn't understand.

Tristan? Who the hell's Tristan? Wait—isn't that the name he called Devon before?

Devon's eyes never left Simon. It was like he couldn't look away even if he wanted to. "You don't know my dad."

Simon's face softened a bit upon hearing his voice. They must have even sounded alike, too. "Oh Devon...if you really believe that, my bet is that *you* don't know your dad."

It wasn't said to be cruel or insulting. It was simply a sad statement of fact. Before it could be contested Simon continued, speaking with a wistfulness that seemed almost tender.

"Tristan Wardell was my best friend. My partner. He was even my roommate for a few years back in London." As bright as they were, his eyes fell suddenly to the table, filled with a kind of sadness that Rae was only beginning to understand. "I loved him like a brother."

The silence that followed this statement was profound. Devon's eyes flickered instinctively to Julian before glassing over, wondering if it could possibly be true.

And then there was one...

There was only a single person left in the circle who had been spared Simon's inquisition. But Rae sensed that he had passed over her on purpose. Focusing on each of the men instead to give her time. Time to figure out how she was supposed to be feeling about all of this. Time to figure out if she wanted to be feeling anything at all.

And it was more time that she desperately needed.

Things were coming apart faster than the group could hold them together. The more Simon unraveled the past, the more they found themselves coming apart at the seams.

It was all a matter of time.

Why hadn't our parents ever mentioned how interconnected they all were? The stories told about the infamous Simon Kerrigan always were so distant, so aloof. Why had no one ever told us how personally connected he was to each and every one of them?

They might need to slow things down in a minute. In fact, they might need to freeze things altogether. And Rae could think of only one person who could do that.

"Where's Angel?" she asked Luke softly, stretching up on her toes so as not to be heard.

Simon had busied himself with the coffee, and both Devon and Julian were staring at each other in that strange way they did when Rae wondered if they were telepathic.

"I don't know," Luke murmured back. "She said she had some things to take care of." He shifted restlessly and glanced out towards the foyer. "I don't want to bail on you guys, but I should go up and check on Molly. Make sure she was actually able to—"

At that moment, there was another knock on the door. It creaked open before anyone could stop it, moving in slow motion as they all stared in terror from the kitchen.

"Knock, knock!" Angel called, her lovely face lit up with a radiant smile. "Look who I happened to find when I raided his apartment in London..."

"Oh shit..." Julian murmured.

The door pushed open wider, and Gabriel's golden head of hair sailed into view.

Rae sucked in a quick breath when she saw him. Tall and handsome. And completely closed off. Just as he had been at the funeral. Just as he had been ever since the day they met.

For a moment both siblings just stood there, glancing around the empty front room. Then they spotted the gang watching them in the kitchen and headed over, clearly having no idea what they were about to find.

Angel danced ahead first, obviously pleased with her efforts. "Turns out, all I needed to do was literally *smoke* him out of the apartment, and..."

She trailed off, coming to a sudden stop in the doorway of the kitchen. Her eyes rested upon Simon and tensed with confusion, like she was trying to recall a vague memory she had worked to suppress.

Simon slowly set his coffee down on the table, staring back with equal wonder. It wasn't until her brother walked into the room behind her that his face lit up with impossible surprise.

"Gabriel?"

Chapter 7

The first time Rae met Gabriel, he was leaning over the bars of her cell. Even from where she was gazing up in the darkness, she could see he was smiling. As if the weight of the entire Privy Council wasn't breathing down his neck. A short time later, he was propositioning her on a fishing boat—shamelessly disregarding her protests as he took off his shirt and climbed into bed. A while after that, he was bleeding—bleeding everywhere. She'd sent him back to London where he'd been strung up and tortured for three days. It wasn't until later that night, passed out on the sofa amongst his new family of friends, that she'd seen him finally let his guard down.

He'd stolen her a birthday cake. Gotten shot in the chest. Both lost and found his humanity all within the same impossible year.

She'd seen him callous, and radiant. Repentant, and cold.

But she had never, *ever* seen him scared.

Until now.

"Gabriel."

The voice hit him like a battering ram, freezing him in his tracks. For a moment, it looked like he was too shocked to move. Too profoundly surprised to do anything other than stare.

Then Simon cried out in delight...and his entire world began to crumble. "It *is* you! I can't believe it!" Simon pushed to his feet, beaming all the while. "Gabriel, you're all grown up!"

All grown up?

Only Simon seemed unaware of the effect his words were having—he was too caught up in the excitement of seeing a living token from his past. But to those who knew him better, the sudden transformation that came over Gabriel couldn't have been more alarming.

Gabriel stumbled backwards. Yes, *stumbled*. His face was pale as a sheet. A thin layer of sweat broke out on his forehead, and when he reached down a hand to steady himself he slipped again.

"Gabriel," Simon tried again, taking a step forward. "It's me, Simon."

That did it. Hearing the name did it.

A broken gasp ripped its way out of Gabriel's chest, and he managed to say only one thing. *"No..."*

Then time seemed to catch up again. The world blinked back into focus, and the kitchen was suddenly a blur of speed.

Angel threw a knife at Simon's heart. Devon grabbed it out of the air.

And Gabriel?

Gabriel bolted from the house.

Without stopping to think, Rae did the only thing that made sense.

She took off after him.

It wasn't easy. A heavy mist had descended over the spacious grounds, and even with a speed tatù on her side it was all she could do to catch up to Gabriel, as he was running like the hounds of hell were behind him. For all she knew, they practically were. She had never seen that expression on a person's face before. Especially his face. Like he'd walked into the kitchen only to come face to face with his own living, breathing nightmare.

He knows my father! She chanted it over and over again. *They've met before! I was right. It all comes back to Cromfield! But why didn't he tell me?! Why would he keep something like that a secret?! My own father!*

Her heart pounded in her chest as she swept over the icy grounds, the tip of her billowing coat skimming the top of the grass. Her hair fell in damp curls around her as she twisted her head this way and that. But still, no Gabriel.

Then she heard him.

Crying.

All her anger and confusion melted clean away as she walked carefully towards him through the fog, approaching as one might approach a frightened child or a wounded animal. His back was towards her and his shoulders hunched as he wept openly into his hands, shivering and trembling in the cold. The sight alone was enough to rip her heart out. It wasn't until she placed a tentative hand on his back that he even noticed she was there.

"I can't breathe," he whispered, sinking down onto the grass. "I can't breathe."

She sank down with him, gathering him up in her arms as he had done for her so many, many times before. Together, they sat there. Rocking back and forth for however long a time. The sun came up and peeked through the morning mist, but they were in a world all to themselves.

Him, closing his eyes as silent tears ran down his face.

Her, running her fingers through his long, golden hair.

It wasn't until his breathing had steadied and his heartbeat had evened out that she even dared to speak. "You knew my father," she said softly. "You've met him before."

His body tensed just at the memory, and for a moment she wished she hadn't spoken.

After an eternity of silence, he nodded. But still, he couldn't bring himself to speak.

She tried again. "At St. Stephen's Church?" she guessed, remembering the place as she had seen it through his memories. "You must have been—"

In a flash, he leapt to his feet.

Gone was the frightened boy who had just wept in her arms. Gone were the emotions that had frozen him with fear, sent him running from the house in a blind panic. They had been replaced with rage. That telltale hardness that had kept him alive since he was a child. Seen him through unspeakable terrors. Looking at him now, she couldn't imagine him crying.

"Yes, Rae. I've *met* your father." He spat out each word like an unholy curse, one that took away a little bit of him just to say it. "I was five years old when he first came to the dungeons. Five years old, but it didn't spare me."

Rae got slowly to her feet, wondering, with a dreadful chill, what exactly that meant.

Gabriel was pacing now, whirling around in tight little circles as if he could shake loose the demons from his past. There was a storm building up inside him. One she couldn't begin to understand.

"He...he's a *bad man*, Rae. You shouldn't have let him into the house."

"They were going to shoot him," she answered quietly. "No arrest. No trial. No accountability. They were going to just shoot him right there as he slept—"

"AND YOU SHOULD HAVE LET THEM!"

The words exploded out of him, lingering in the fog.

For a second, the two of them just stood there. Gabriel, panting as if he'd run a marathon. Rae, standing perfectly still.

If there was one thing Gabriel could be counted on, it was total honesty. He didn't feel the need to censor himself the way other people did. Didn't feel the need to sugar-coat the truth to make it more palatable for the masses. Call it his traumatic upbringing inside a lunatic's cave. Call it his natural born aversion to sanctimonious bullshit.

Ever since he'd burst into her life, Gabriel was the only person Rae could trust to tell her the absolute truth. Never coddling or shielding her the way the others tried. Trusting that, no matter how hard it was to hear, she could handle it.

It was one of the reasons she was so terrified right now.

"You really believe that." As strong as she tried to make it, her voice came out as no more than a whisper. "You really believe that he deserves to die."

She didn't ask it as a question. One look at Gabriel's face told her that there was no question. But just in case there was the slightest bit of doubt, his green eyes locked onto hers.

"Give me a gun...and I'll do it myself."

She didn't doubt him. Not for a second. In fact, she'd seen him make the exact same threat the last time a person he loved was in danger. He didn't hesitate to pull the trigger.

And now she'd brought a man into their house who was a threat to them all.

"I'm sorry," she said quietly. When he glanced up, she shook her head with a sigh. "I'm sorry for whatever he did to you—"

"Don't!" He threw up a hand in between them. "Don't apologize for him! Don't act like this is something you can apologize for! You need to *fix* this. *Now.* You need to get him out of here!"

"And where's he supposed to go?" she exclaimed. "How am I supposed to deal in these kinds of absolutes? How am I supposed to sentence my own family?"

"Family?!" Gabriel grabbed reflexively at his arm, as if it had been burned. "Why the hell do you think I never told you?" he demanded, his eyes shining with unspeakable rage. "Why do you think I kept secret all the things he'd done?"

He was flat-out yelling now. The darkest words coming from the fiercest kind of love.

"Who should have to know their father is capable of something like that?! Who should have to know they're the offspring of a monster?!"

Rae froze where she stood. Feeling as though he'd slapped her.

All this time, all these years...he's been keeping the biggest secret of all.

But it was as he said. He hadn't been doing it for himself. He'd been doing it for her. To protect her. Just as she needed to protect him now.

"You're not a murderer, Gabriel." She wasn't sure of many things these days, but of this she was certain. "You're not going to kill a man in cold blood."

For a moment, he just stared at her. The wind blew his hair around him, and despite the terrible threat hanging in the air between them he suddenly looked very much like a child.

Then his face hardened, and the light died in his eyes.

"Who do you think taught me how?"

Then he was off.

Off before she could stop him. Off before she'd even decided if she should. She stared after him helplessly, frozen in place, until a single thought propelled her forward.

I can't let him do this to himself!

It was as if the ground itself had released her. Before she knew what was happening she was flying back over the frosty grass, closing the distance between them.

Simon Kerrigan might deserve the worst the world had to offer. He might even deserve to die. But Gabriel was not going to be the one to pull the trigger. The man had taken enough from him already. He wasn't going to take that, too.

"Gabriel, *wait!*"

He was almost to the house now. The sight of it only spurred him on faster. He didn't have a weapon of any sort, didn't have a gun. But they both knew he didn't need one. If Gabriel wanted someone dead, he need only think it.

"*Gabriel!*"

For a split second, she thought she wasn't going to make it. Even with her using Riley's cheetah tatù, he had gotten too much of a head start. But then the front door opened, and Devon ran outside.

The two men sprinted on an intercept course, colliding in the middle of the field.

"Gabriel, you don't want to do this." Devon caught him lightly by the arms, and eased him back away from the house. "Trust me. You'll regret it in the morning. Just take a second to think."

Gabriel ripped his arms away, enraged beyond reason yet eerily calm. "The only thing I'm going to *regret*," he spat, "is letting that man breathe for a second longer than is required." He glanced up at the house, eyes dilating as if they could see through the ivy-covered stone. "Simon Kerrigan is going to die today. He should've died a long time ago."

He tried again to move forward, but Devon held him back. It was the fight Rae had never wanted to see happen. One the two men had been dancing around since the day they first met.

"Devon," Gabriel looked him square in the eyes, "stand aside."

It looked like Devon wanted to. In fact, it looked like a part of him was ready to march inside and pull the trigger himself. But Devon's sense of morality had never been as flexible as Gabriel's was. Especially when it came to things that could do Rae potential harm.

His brown eyes shone with sympathy, even as he shook his head. "You know I can't do that, man. Come on, let's just take a breath—"

The punch came out of nowhere, hitting him right in the eye. It made contact just as Rae came flying up behind them in the grass. She saw the first of the blood trickle down Devon's cheek.

"Gabriel!" she shrieked. "What the hell are you doing?!"

She rushed in between them, but Devon never moved. He looked neither upset nor particularly surprised. Instead, he was staring at Gabriel with a look of unthinkable pity.

"You're not going to do that to Rae," he said quietly. Half as a vote of confidence, half as a command. "You're not going to make her watch her own father die."

Gabriel gritted his teeth together, seemingly unaware that his hands had started shaking. "I don't want to hurt you—"

"Then don't," Devon replied simply. He wiped away the blood with the back of his sleeve, pushing Rae discreetly aside in the process. "Let's go into town and get a beer."

Go into town and get a beer? That was his grand solution?

Rae turned to him in absolute shock, but Gabriel was staring like he'd never quite seen him before. His lips parted uncertainly, and for a moment he almost looked tempted. Then the distant hum of voices echoed from the house, and his face hardened once more.

"Move."

This time, Devon seemed to realize the time for words had passed. He braced himself ever so casually in the grass and spoke to Rae, keeping his eyes on Gabriel the entire time. "Honey, go inside."

"Are you kidding me?!"

She threw herself in between them once more, unable to comprehend how things had gotten away from her so quickly. One minute, Gabriel was crying on her shoulder, vulnerable and helpless as a child. The next, he was preparing to beat her fiancé into the ground.

"Guys, you cannot actually be ready to—"

Then *she* was flying through the air.

It was the last thing the boys did together, throwing her at the same time out of harm's reach.

Then they turned to each other.

"STOP!"

But it was no use trying to stop it. It would be over before she even landed on the ground.

Of all the men in the world, Devon and Gabriel had to be the most dangerous pairing. Not only because of the skill and impossible strength with which they fought, but because of the devastating speed with which it was done.

Devon got in five hits. Five hits in under a second. Five hits that would have leveled a normal person to the ground. Except Gabriel wasn't exactly what you'd call normal.

Despite not have the enhanced abilities of Devon's tatù, Gabriel had grown up fighting in a slightly different way. He'd grown up fighting for his life. It was something you couldn't unlearn.

"*GABRIEL—NO!*"

There was no more fighting now. No more maneuvers. Devon had frozen so suddenly it was like the whole thing had never even happened. If it wasn't for the look of exquisite pain rippling across his handsome face, she would have thought he'd simply given up. That, and the fact that Gabriel was standing just a foot in front of him, holding up two lethal fingers.

"*GABRIEL!*"

She had seen him do that just one time before. Seen him twitch his fingers and take a man's life into his hands. Seen him slowly reverse the flow of blood to the heart.

Her feet touched down just as Devon fell to his knees. Then she was racing forward.

Her body flipped through a dozen different tatùs as she tore across the grass. Each more deadly than the next. Electricity, speed, kinetic vibrations...fire.

It shocked her, then didn't shock her all at the same time. That her body would have instinctively settled on the one thing she needed most. To save the love of her life. To stop the man intent on hurting him. Coincidentally, it was the only tatù Gabriel couldn't possibly survive.

Blue flames laced up the sides of her arms, like angelic wings trailing out behind her. But the second she got back to the clearing, she saw that, once again, she was too late.

It was over.

Devon was still kneeling on the grass, but it wasn't at Gabriel's mercy. He was in a state of momentary shock, pulling in silent gasps as he tried to catch his breath.

Gabriel was a different story.

"I can't...I can't believe I just..." He stared down at his hands in sheer astonishment, like he couldn't fathom what he'd just seen them do. His voice faltered and he lifted his eyes, looking suddenly small. "I can't believe I just did that."

The three of them never mentioned what happened in the clearing that day. Even in the immediate aftermath with each other... they never said a word.

As soon as Devon was able to stand without help they headed back inside, only to find that Simon had been successfully relocated to the basement. The tatù-inhibitors from the boathouse had also been relocated and the problem had been successfully, if only temporarily, put out of sight.

There was no more talk of killing Simon. Whether or not the desire still remained, Gabriel had also put it successfully, if only temporarily, out of sight.

That moment with Devon had been a wake-up call, a warning of a line that could never be uncrossed. It was a lesson Gabriel was unlikely to forget anytime soon.

But while the drive to fight had been eliminated, the one to flee had increased tenfold.

Twice, Gabriel tried to carry Angel away from the house, slinging her over his shoulder despite her pounding fists and protests. Twice, Rae and Devon found him frozen on the driveway. When Gabriel realized he wasn't making any headway he actually tried dragging Julian along as well, as if that would convince her.

The strange siblings battled for the better part of an hour, but made little headway. Gabriel was clearly unwilling to leave Angel alone in the house, and Angel was clearly unwilling to go.

In the end, Gabriel simply pulled up a chair and sat at the top of the basement stairs, staring unblinkingly at the door.

As much as Rae wanted to hover in the shadows, monitoring his every move, she knew the danger had momentarily passed. The incident in the field had awoken something deep inside him, reminding him that he still had something to lose.

Besides...there was another man in the house who required her attention.

"Hey." She flashed Devon a quick smile as she slipped inside their bedroom. He was standing with his back to her, rifling through a dresser drawer for a new shirt. "Stripping, are we?"

He grinned, but kept his eyes on his task. "I got blood on the other one. Didn't want anyone downstairs to start asking questions."

Rae opened her mouth, but found herself unable to speak. Their light banter had gotten them through a number of tense situations, but the images in her mind were still too fresh.

"Hey, come here." Devon saw the look on her face, and gathered her quickly into his arms. He smelled of grass and blood. A strange combination, but a comforting one nonetheless. She breathed it in deeply as she closed her eyes.

"I was so scared," she murmured. "I thought for a second that he—"

"Gabriel was just lost." He stroked the back of her hair, his eyes faraway in thought. "He's been broken more ways than I thought were possible. Everything was stripped away."

Rae pulled in a shaky breath, haunted with the memory of his tear-stained face.

"But he's built something here as well," Devon continued thoughtfully. "He has a life now, a family, a home. He just needed someone to help him remember that."

She paused for a moment, thinking.

"So you volunteered yourself as a ritual sacrifice?"

An involuntary shudder rippled through Devon's body. "No...I didn't think he was going to do that."

They pulled back at the same time, and he flashed her a quirky grin.

"So you decided to light the guy on fire?"

She hesitated, then buried her face back in his chest. "No...I didn't think I was going to do that, either."

Chapter 8

The rest of the day grew intentionally subdued.

Molly dozed fitfully as Luke read parenting books beside her. Spared from his impromptu kidnapping, Julian had gone for that drive after all—Angel riding shotgun. In a most uncharacteristic move, Devon had passed out for a few hours on the bed. Apparently, having one's blood held hostage could do that to you.

And amid working out her great plan after the discovery of Simon Kerrigan, Rae realized there was something she couldn't put off for even a second longer.

She was going to have to talk to Simon Kerrigan.

For their first official father-daughter conversation, she selected her clothing carefully. Head-to-toe black. Reminiscent of the Privy Council. Respectful of the *actual* father she'd just lost. No skin to make contact. No color open to interpretation.

Likewise, she swept her hair up into a simple ponytail. She looked enough like her mother without the added benefit of her tumbling raven locks. She'd already caught Simon staring at them in the kitchen, and the last thing she needed was an unnecessary distraction.

She wore no makeup. No jewelry. No ornamentation or frills. After using it as the final nail in Cromfield's coffin, Rae had locked her engagement ring away in the drawer of her nightstand. She couldn't bear to tell her heartsick mother that she was soon to get the happy ending that they had always wanted. At least not yet.

She finished dressing quickly, and stared at her reflection in the mirror. Perhaps she was imagining it...in fact, she would *have* to be imagining it, since it was only a short time ago that her brother, Kraigan, had stripped away her troublesome immortality—but she could have sworn that she looked different. Older, somehow. Or perhaps, a strange kind of tired. The kind that couldn't be cured by just a few nights' sleep. The kind that required complete and utter absolution.

Then, all that was left to do was wait.

After the rest of the house had fallen asleep she tiptoed downstairs, careful not to wake Devon when she left. It wasn't often that she could slip past him undetected, but his brush with Gabriel's tatù had taken more out of him than he was willing to admit. He was still passed out cold when she pushed open the door and ghosted outside to the hall.

Despite the late hour, every light was still shining brightly. Just as they had done every night since the gang had moved into the house. For a moment, she was tempted to turn them off. If for no other reason than to spare them from a massive electricity bill. But as soon as she lifted her finger to the switch, her hand fell back to her side and she continued on her way.

Maybe tomorrow night. Or the night after that.

The house had three levels. Four, if you counted the attic. She descended to the ground floor quickly, and then hurried down the back hallway to the door that led down to the basement.

Gabriel was still sitting at the top of the stairs.

"Oh!" She clutched her chest and fell back a step when she saw him. "Sorry. I didn't know that you were still...what are you doing here?"

He hadn't moved a single inch since the second he'd sat down—over nine hours ago. If she didn't know better, she'd swear he had used some sort of self-freezing charm. A defensive sort of ink that would render him a perfect statue.

His eyes flashed up, flickering briefly over her carefully selected wardrobe before coming to rest on her face. "I could ask you the same question."

A blossom of heat rose in her cheeks, and she reached up automatically to fiddle with hair that was no longer there. "Actually, I was just...I mean... I was just checking on..."

His lips twitched up into the ghost of a smile. "Are we going to play this game?"

She let out a quiet sigh. "I'm going to talk to him, Gabriel."

For a second, his muscles tensed at the ready. Then, with what looked like a visible effort, he relaxed them with a nod. "I figured you might."

Her eyebrows lifted, and she took a step back in surprise. If she'd known Gabriel was still sitting watch, she would have expected the inquisition. At the best, a reprimand the likes of which she would never forget. At the worst, a reenactment of his 'forced relocation' stunt from earlier that afternoon. Truth be told, if she'd known that Gabriel was still sitting watch, she would have put off this conversation altogether for a later time.

"You *figured* I might?" she repeated incredulously, taking a tentative step forward. "Is this some kind of trick? Are you about to throw a bag over my head and lock me away in your trunk for safe-keeping?"

He pushed stiffly to his feet, stretching out his long limbs. "It isn't like you to avoid something because it makes you uncomfortable. And I've never known you to hide away from the tough conversations just because they were tough." He cocked his head towards the front door. "Case in point."

They flashed back at the same time. Not to the near-catastrophic events that had followed, but to the time they had spent earlier. Sitting together on the icy grass. Catching their breath in the silence, before eventually trying to talk it through.

If only it had ended there.

Gabriel seemed to be thinking the same thing. He dropped his eyes to the floor and headed down the hall. Presumably to set up his watch at a further distance so she could have a little privacy. But just before rounding the corner, he suddenly paused. "Rae, about Devon—"

"He made his choice," she said briskly, unwilling to discuss it, "and so did you. It's over now. Nothing left to talk about."

He held her gaze for a second more before nodding abruptly and turning around. It wasn't until he'd reached the end of the hall that Rae called out once more. "Gabriel, if you ever touch him again..."

His face whitened. Not at her threat, but at the memory of what he'd done. His jaw clenched and he glanced over his shoulder, a promise rising to his lips. "I'd do it myself."

A few weeks ago, she might not have believed him. A few *days* ago, she might not have believed him. But looking at him now? She couldn't have been more sure.

The epic battle between Devon Wardell and Gabriel Alden was finally over.

He disappeared around the corner and proceeded to the living room, flipping off the lights as he went. She almost called out to tell him to stop and then caught her breath. She turned with great trepidation to the basement door. She had felt so prepared upstairs, done anything she could think of to make herself ready. But now that the moment was upon her, the only urge she felt was to run away.

Except you don't run away from the tough conversations, remember?

A chill ran through her shoulders as she lifted her fingers to the knob.

What the hell was he talking about? Of course I do.

Before she could talk herself out of it, she took a deep breath and pushed open the door, peering down the dimly-lit stairs to the man sitting in a chair at the base. *Will he ask me about my* tatù? *Ask to see what it looks like?*

The second Simon saw her, his entire face came alive with a long-awaited smile.

"It's about time." He gazed steadily up at her. "I imagine there are some questions you'd like to ask me..."

"Why shouldn't I have let my guards shoot you?"

Simon blinked, taken aback by the directness of her query. They were sitting in opposite chairs—granted, he was strapped into his. And with the iridescent lightbulb dangling above them, the entire thing felt a good deal more like an interrogation than a conversation.

But as well-trained as his daughter might have been in the art of information extraction, he had been taught the same lessons decades before.

With a wry smile, Simon shifted in his chair to slow down their pace. "I suppose it depends on who you ask."

She didn't blink. "I'm asking you."

Father and daughter shared a look.

"I know what you want me to say," he said quietly. "You want me to say that you should have done it. That you should have pulled the trigger yourself. You want me to say that I deserve it."

"Would that be true?" Rae asked stiffly, sitting rigid as a board in her chair. "Do you think that you deserve it?"

Simon paused for a second before leaning back with a twinkling smile. "Tell you what—I'll make you a deal. I'll answer your questions, and I'll answer them truthfully. But for every question I answer, you have to answer a question of mine."

Rae fell silent, considering the proposal. It wasn't what she had planned on but, truth be told, she had very few expectations when it came to what Simon would or would not do. There was little harm in satisfying his curiosities, and if it would lead to the satisfaction of her own? Plus, she knew what kind of questions he was going to ask. "Fine."

"Excellent!" Simon clapped his hands together. "In honor of your participation, I'll even volunteer to go first. In answer to your first question..." his smile faded, "...yes. I deserve it."

The room grew abruptly still.

"You do?" Rae shivered in spite of herself, searching his eyes for any hint of a lie. "You really think you deserve to die?"

Simon's face grew thoughtful. "The man I was before, the man I was ten years ago...yes, I believe he deserved to die. The things he did, the people he hurt—the world would have been a better place without him."

The things *he* did? The people *he* hurt?

"You're awfully quick to disassociate yourself." Rae's eyes narrowed slightly. "Pronouns can't save you here. You did those things yourself. No matter how wide your perspective."

"Well, prison gives that to you."

"What?"

"Perspective."

The entire exchange came out a lot quicker than either of them had intended, and Rae leaned back in her chair, slowing things down a notch. "Alright, well...do you think the person you are now deserves the same punishment?"

"Not so fast." He stopped her with a smile. "It's my turn."

While she shifted restlessly in front of him, he laced his fingers beneath his chin, studying her with intense curiosity. "Do you like pancakes?"

For a second, she almost laughed. Then she caught herself. "Do I like...pancakes?" Her eyebrows lifted delicately. "Really? That's your question?"

Simon's face warmed. "When you were a child, I couldn't get you to eat them for the life of me. I tried everything I could think of. Threats. Bribes. Telling you that your mother made them instead. It didn't matter what I did. Every time I put them on your plate, they'd end up on the wall."

It took Rae a second to realize she wasn't breathing. Her body had gone very still and she was watching him with rapt attention, hanging on his every word.

"Beth said it was just a phase. Promised me that you'd come around eventually. But you were always a stubborn child, and I'd be willing to bet *that* hasn't changed. So, my question to you is simple: do you, or do you not, like pancakes?"

A single tear tingled at the corner of Rae's eye, but she brushed it away using her best speed tatù. Odds were, Simon never even saw. "I don't like pancakes."

It wasn't true. She happened to like them very much. But for whatever reason, she was suddenly sure she was never going to eat one again.

"My turn." She collected herself quickly, and looked him right in the eyes. "When you married my mother, a woman with a particularly powerful tatù, was that all just an act?"

It was said directly enough, and the silent implication was clear.

Was I just another entry for your wicked diary? Was my entire existence just one of your games?

Simon's eyes tightened, and for a moment the playful charade fell away. All the witty back-and-forth came to an abrupt stop as his face darkened with a heartbreaking nostalgia. "I loved your mother," he murmured. "I loved her with all of my heart. Even at the very end, after I'd found out what she'd done... I never stopped loving her. Or you."

He tagged it on as an afterthought, but the two words caught in Rae's teeth. She tried very hard to maintain a neutral expression, but it was getting harder and harder to stay distant.

"Are you dating one of the boys I met today?"

The sudden frivolity shocked her, and for a moment she was too stunned to speak. The guilty silence that followed gave her away.

Simon nodded sagely, running back through the roster in his mind. "Which one?"

Rae's head jerked to the side, and she back-pedaled quickly. "That's two questions."

Simon let out a bark of laughter. "That doesn't mean you don't have to answer either—"

"Did you murder my grandparents?"

The back and forth stopped abruptly as the conversation took a sudden turn.

"No." Simon gave her a hard look. "*That* was Jonathon Cromfield."

Funny he should mention him...

Rae sucked in a quick breath as the question she had most wanted to ask floated to the surface of her mind. It went beyond interrogation and mind games. It even went beyond the shock of seeing her long-dead father. It was something that had plagued her for as long as she could remember. Haunting her since she was only just a child.

"You were working with Cromfield—for however long a time. Doing the same kinds of experiments, trying to develop the same kinds of serums."

"That's not a question, Rae."

"You kidnapped people. Tortured them. Treated them like lab rats until they were too used up to do anything but die."

"Again—not a question."

"You traded one life for another, played God—"

He shifted with a tad of impatience. "If you're trying to ask me why I did it, then the answer is that I had everything to gain and nothing left to lose—"

"You had ME."

An unexpected surge of emotion coursed through her body, sending shockwaves through her legs, and sporadic shivers through her arms. The fairy on her lower back seemed to burn with long-awaited rage, and no matter how hard she tried to stay neutral it was impossible to keep the hate and bitter resentment from leaking into her voice.

"You had me," she said again, quieter this time. "And Mom. You had a *family*, Simon. *Something to lose.*" She quoted his own words back to him, shaming him where he sat. "So, yeah—my question stands: how the hell could you do it?"

They sat in silence for a long time.

So long that Rae didn't think he was going to answer. But just as she was about to push to her feet he shook his head, an indecipherable emotion shadowing across his face.

"In a way... I felt like I was doing it *for* you." His eyes fixed on the floor, clouding with things long since passed. "For Beth as well. I thought I was giving the two of you a future. Ridding the world of corruption. Creating the kind of place where no one had to be afraid. Where no one had to hide."

The kind of place where you ruled as tyrannical overlord, right? Where every knee had to bow to you?

She didn't say it out loud. At this point, it didn't much matter. The man was clearly at least partially insane. Broken in a way you couldn't fix with words in a basement. Broken in a way you could only contain.

"Last question." He looked at her suddenly, a flicker of that old curiosity lighting up the dark centers of his eyes. "What kind of tatù did you get?"

At that, Rae pushed to her feet with a wry smile. The conversation was over. And, to be honest, she wasn't sure if it had helped more or hurt more.

"Where are you going?" he asked quickly as she headed for the door. His legs tensed up to follow, before falling back under the weight of their ties.

Rae simply shook her head as she pulled open the door. "You see, Simon, you just answered *my* last question."

The light flipped off.

She felt her own voice harden as she spoke, "How long could you go before asking about my ink?"

Chapter 9

As imminent as the problem was, the next morning couldn't be about Simon Kerrigan.

Rae woke, got dressed, brushed her teeth, and set out to do the last thing one wants to do when harboring an international fugitive. She went to meet with the heads of state.

"Are you sure you don't want me to come with you?"

Rae glanced over her shoulder in surprise from where she'd been buttoning up her blouse at the vanity. She hadn't realized that Devon was awake as well, but sure enough, he sat propped up against the headboard—watching her with a look of thoughtful concern.

"Hey there, how'd you sleep?" She deflected his question, crossing the room to perch on the bed beside him. He was always the most handsome like this, she thought. Having just woken, still dazed and tousled from sleep. Without thinking about it, she reached out to stroke his dark hair away from his face. "I didn't even hear you wake up."

The corner of his mouth twitched up in a half-smile. "I have an internal alarm that goes off whenever you're getting dressed. It's a guy thing—you wouldn't understand."

She giggled softly, then louder as he wrapped his arms around her waist and pulled her back down onto the bed. "Don't! Devon, *don't*—I'm serious! You'll mess up my hair!"

He paused, but didn't release her. Instead, he merely spun her around so she was lying on top of his chest instead. "I'll mess up your hair?" he quoted incredulously. "What—are you and Molly channeling now? You don't have some big news you're waiting to tell me, right?"

"Yeah," Rae snorted, "because that's exactly what we need right now: a baby."

Devon tilted his head to the side, his brown eyes twinkling with amusement. "I don't think it would be so bad. A miniature replication of the two of us. My winning charm and your innate clumsiness wrapped up into one little package."

"Really? Your winning charm, and my *innate clumsiness*?" Rae countered, smacking him on the chest. "You really think that's going to be my only contribution?"

Devon shuddered dramatically. "I can only hope! Let's be honest, babe, it's not like we want you passing along those cooking skills..."

"*Hey!*" Rae burst out laughing, despite her best efforts to appear mad. "I'll have you know that you should be so lucky for me to be the mother of your child! Someone has to balance out that giant savior complex the poor thing is going to inherit."

But Devon didn't take offense. He was dreaming now. Tilting his head lazily back towards the ceiling as a thousand unexplored possibilities danced behind his eyes. "Molly will dress it like a doll. We'll take it to Scotland on the weekends." He glanced over matter-of-factly. "We'll have to name it after Julian, of course."

Rae only grinned. "Of course."

"Holidays in London, vacations in France. Who knows, if we're feeling benevolent, we may even name Kraigan as godfather."

"*Kraigan?!*"

The two of them burst into simultaneous laughter before falling abruptly silent. Shuddering at the ghastly mental image.

"You know, probably best not even to joke about that one," Rae advised.

"Yeah," Devon frowned, "I didn't think it through..."

She flashed him a grin and made to get up, but he caught her gently by the arms, shifting higher up on the pillows as he started buttoning her shirt instead.

"Let me do that," he murmured, taking his time with each one. "You always do it wrong."

Rae's eyebrows lifted suggestively, as his hand 'accidentally' slipped beneath the fabric.

"Oh, *I* do, is that right?" A trail of goosebumps followed his fingers as they stroked up her skin. "It wouldn't happen to have anything to do with this internal alarm of yours, would it?"

His eyes widened with perfect innocence as he shook his head.

Perfect, adorable, *mischievous* innocence. The kind that barely hid his dimples.

"Great," she muttered, casting a martyred look at the ceiling, "that's something else I can look forward to in a child. That damn look—they'll get away with everything."

He grinned. "Not with a psychic uncle, a lightning-throwing aunt, and a fire-wielding grandmother they won't. Not to mention their grandfather."

Rae caught her breath, and his fingers froze in place as he realized his mistake.

"I meant my dad," he said quickly. "My dad's the dean of the school. I just meant, it'll be weird for them at Guilder."

The playful mood vanished right there on the spot, and Rae finished up the rest of her shirt by herself. She was just putting on some pearl earrings, staring at her reflection back at the vanity, when Devon came up behind her in the mirror.

"I'm sorry," he murmured, kissing the top of her shoulder. "I didn't mean to upset you."

She forced a tight smile and shook her head. "Not your fault. Not a bit of it is even remotely your fault."

He hesitated for another second, staring at her reflection in the mirror before venturing, "How did it go with him last night?" The locket she'd been fastening around her neck slipped from her fingers in surprise, and he caught it with lightning hands. "Innate clumsiness..."

But she ignored the teasing jab, turning around with genuine shock.

"How did you know that I went to talk with him? You were out cold."

He gazed down at her with an amused kind of pity. "Out so cold that I wouldn't notice my fiancée leaving the bed when there's a psychopath staying in the house? Sorry, love, no such luck."

Rae grinned faintly and stared down at her hands, wondering where she should even begin.

On the one hand, she was grateful he hadn't tried to stop her. Hadn't insisted that he go with her or, at the least, stand guard. In a lot of ways, that was a very different version of Devon than the one she'd grown up with. Their relationship had evolved, as had their ability to trust.

On the other hand, she had nothing good to report. No 'good news' or glimmer of hope that was going to ease the burden of her decision.

Simon Kerrigan was the same confusing, charming, duplicitous, murderous, ink-obsessed man he had always been. Nothing had changed, and no matter how many times he insisted otherwise she wasn't sure if anything ever could.

On the other hand, he'd asked her if she liked pancakes.

"He's...complicated," she summarized vaguely, head spinning as it raced back to replay his every word. It wasn't the first time she had done so that morning, not by any means. No matter how bewildering or chilling those words might have been, they belonged to her father.

Every moment, every answer... it was one that she'd never expected to have.

Devon seemed to intuit this, and graciously chose not to press the matter any further. "I would imagine." He fastened the locket with a sweep of his fingers, and kissed her once more on the back of the neck. "Are you sure you don't want me to come with you? You never answered when I asked before."

She slipped on her jacket with a sigh.

There was nothing in the *world* she wanted more. Governmental formalities had never been her strong suit to begin with, and despite having been voted president against her will, that instinctive diplomacy hadn't sprung up overnight. Truth be told, Devon had always been much better at that sort of thing than she was, but as much as she'd like to bring him along it was far more important that he remain at the house.

"I wish," she groaned, already bracing herself against what was to come, "but you need to stay here. For better or worse, Simon's still locked up in the basement. And if yesterday is any indication as to how the rest of them are taking the news... I'd feel a lot more comfortable if you were here to keep the peace. On both sides."

The weight of that responsibility couldn't be overstated, but true to form Devon just flashed her an easy smile. "Then I'll stay."

How did I get so lucky? How is this the man I wake up to every morning? Her face relaxed into a genuine smile as she stretched up on her toes to kiss him goodbye. "Thank you."

They stayed like that for a moment. Him, carefully avoiding disturbing her curls. Her, stalling the moment of inevitable departure. Then, when she could put it off no longer, she finally headed out to the hallway, high heels clicking on the wooden floor.

"See you soon!" she called over her shoulder.

"Good luck!"

It wasn't until she'd almost made it to the stairs that she suddenly doubled back, poking her head through the door to see him dressing for the day as well. "You really think about what it would be like to have a kid?"

His eyes twinkled for a moment before growing ominously dark. "We'd have to be careful about its tatù. With our luck, it would probably turn out like some kind of Lisa Frank creation gone wrong..."

Rae snorted and headed back down the hall. "Goodbye, Devon."

"A sparkling fairy riding a fox..."

No matter how slowly Rae tried to drive, it seemed like no time at all before she saw the iron gates of her old school.

That's what happens when your fiancé is obsessed with sports cars.

A heavy feeling settled in the pit of her stomach as she slowed down at the gate to be waved inside. It seemed like just yesterday she was driving in here for the first time. She had been on a bus, then. A normal bus, thinking that she was going to a normal school.

Little did she know how things would begin to unravel...

"Morning, Madame President."

It wasn't Charlie this time, but Chuck. The alternate guard, who might share a formal name with the first, but would give you hell if you ever mixed them up.

"Morning... Chuck," Rae replied, catching herself at the last moment. "I'm just here for the meeting with Fodder and Keene."

The metal divider lifted at once.

"Of course, go right on through. I think you're the last one to arrive, actually."

Perfect, Rae thought as she sped down the drive. *Just perfect.*

There hadn't been some great ceremony the day she'd been told about the election. There hadn't been any pomp and circumstance, nothing at all to distinguish it from any other day. Time was a blur after the great battle. Truth be told, Rae hadn't even known that the surviving members of the Council had already scheduled a vote for Carter's replacement. It seemed like she was just hanging up her dress from the funeral when she got the call.

They had done it in a basement. Her mother's basement, in fact.

The rest of the house was still being used as a makeshift hospital. When you stage a war between two magical armies, people aren't the only casualties you will accrue. The factory itself had been half-collapsed in the process. While that meant a hasty letter of explanation to the local city officials, it also meant that a good deal of those injured were trapped under the rubble, meaning that the excavation process and the treatment to follow trickled in slowly. No sooner had the door of the Scottish farm house shut for the 'last time,' than it would burst open again, echoed by frantic shouts and trails of blood as brother carried in sister. Father carried in son.

Rae had no particular skills to combat the insurgence of the sick and wounded. Alicia's talent as a diagnostician was still well beyond her reach, so the most she could do was conjure. Gauze, tape, needles, drugs. After that it was hospital cots, curtains, wheelchairs, and crutches and casts.

At one point, she and the rest of the gang had even donated blood. Sitting in a silent circle where the television used to be. Ironically, it had been on that day that Louis Keene walked into the house, followed closely by Luke's father. Rae still had trouble thinking of him as the Commander of the Knights, despite having seen him on the battlefield herself.

She hadn't been given an option. She hadn't been given a choice. Truth be told, she hadn't even been given time for a reaction before she was whisked off to Guilder. A rallying point around which the new government was soon to convene.

In just the short time since the first of the coffins were laid in the ground, she'd already overseen three formal gatherings and conducted numerous matters of state. This gathering today was meant to be the fourth. It was one she was already dreading as she parked in her usual spot behind the Oratory and started trudging up the grass.

Sure enough, she was the last to arrive.

Her cheeks flushed pink and she felt relieved that she had at least preemptively combatted her lack of punctuality with something as formal as pearls as she skidded around the side of the table and took a seat. She might be late, but at least she was dressed like a professional.

"Morning," she murmured, keeping her eyes on the packet of paper that had been laid out in front of her. "Bit of traffic today..."

"Rae?"

She looked up swiftly, her body relaxing in automatic relief. Despite the new formalities and titles that had been foisted upon her, Mr. Fodder was the only one to continue to address her by her first name. It was even more out of character for him than for most—the man liked things in their proper place—but he must have sensed that she needed a kind of ally right now. He was a parent, after all. And, for better or worse, it was something that Carter would have done.

"Yes?"

Were they finished already? Perhaps they had just started without her!

"You're in Carmine's chair." He saw her look of blank confusion, and gestured kindly to the head of the table. "Perhaps you'd like to sit in your own?"

Ally indeed! Carter would have been happy that she had sat down at all.

"Oh. Right." She shut her folder—Carmine's folder—with a surge of embarrassment and sat down quickly in the required chair.

Was it her imagination, or was this chair a little smaller than the rest? It seemed like the rest of the men were towering down over her. And the heat. Had someone turned up the heat in the little room? It had to be at least ninety degrees...

"We thought we'd begin today by scheduling a formal time to make the announcement of your election to the royal family."

Okay. What about these lights? She could barely see anything going on around her with this spotlight blazing down.

"The...the royal family?" She fiddled nervously with her locket, pulling it away from her neck. Felt like the freakin' thing had her in a stranglehold. "Is that really necessary?"

Keene leaned forward with a polite smile. "I'm afraid it is. The Privy Council has maintained close ties with Palace since its creation in the time of Henry VIII. We generally make it a custom to inform them when power switches hands. Especially in such...such unusual circumstances."

For a second, the entire room went dead still. Rae's eyes zeroed in on the table, and she could hear every beat of her heart as it pulsed behind her eyes.

Then, just a second later, things moved on. They had a depressing way of moving on.

"If I understand it correctly, you and the future Queen of England already share a passing acquaintance?" Keene continued quickly, striving to keep things going.

"Yes," Rae said quickly, stacking then re-stacking the papers in front of her, just to give her something to do with her hands. "We drag-raced through the countryside just a few weeks ago."

There was a pause.

"That... *and* a lot of other more acceptable things..."

If only Victor Mallins could see me now. It would have been his finest hour.

"Of course," Keene said, with a hint of confusion. Sitting on his other side, Rae could have sworn that Mr. Fodder stifled a faint smile. "Well, at any rate, she and the Crown Prince will have to be informed. We can send a formal envoy—"

"Or I can just text her." Rae took out her phone and laid it tentatively on the table. A dozen pairs of eyes locked onto it like it was the devil incarnate. A symbolic downfall to their beloved, if somewhat antiquated, traditions. "I'd promise to use a really nice font..."

"I'll take care of the election notice," Fodder swooped in swiftly, saving Keene the issue of having to come up with a response. "And if I'm not mistaken, that actually concludes our business here." He gave Rae a faint smile, sensing her scarcely-contained delight. "That is, unless you had anything to report after having cleared the cells in the factory—"

"What?" Rae went suddenly rigid, gripping the edge of the table in front of her. "What do you mean? What would I have to report?"

Fodder paused, looking her over curiously. "Well nothing, I expect. It was just a cursory inspection—"

"Good." She pushed quickly to her feet. "Well, then, if that's all, gentlemen, I think we're finished here."

The rest of the room pushed back their chairs as well, shooting each other sideways glances as they nodded a polite farewell and headed to the door. Rae watched them go with that same sickly feeling in her stomach, feeling like, for the fourth time, she had somehow failed them.

More importantly, feeling like she had somehow failed Carter.

"It *will* get easier." Fodder was the last to go, gazing around the empty room before gesturing her out ahead of him. "I promise."

Rae flashed him a weak smile, but shook her head. "I don't see how it could possibly get any worse."

He chuckled, holding open the door. "You should've seen some of my first meetings when I was first elected Commander of the Knights. Trust me, Rae. You're doing just fine."

"I'm a quarter of most of their ages," she muttered under her breath, nodding politely at a cluster still lingering in the Oratory. "How am I supposed to 'take charge' when out of every person in the room I'm the one with the least experience?"

"*You're* the one they elected," he said firmly, pushing open the double-doors and heading out with her to the parking lot. "For better or worse, you're their chosen leader. And I wouldn't say you have the least experience. In fact, when it comes to rallying an entire community to action, I'd say you might even have the most."

She glanced up at him. "Not more than you."

He laughed again, sounding very much like his son. "Well, not every leader can be as naturally gifted and experienced as me."

She couldn't help but grin as they made their way through the lot.

Ever since Fodder had found out that he was going to be a grandfather, just a few short days after the battle, it seemed like his entire perspective on life had changed. Gone was the man who never smiled. The man who valued precision and order above all else. He had been replaced with someone Rae hardly even recognized. Someone who unbuttoned his collar and dared to come to work without a tie. Someone who made jokes and laughed in a voice just like his son. Someone who stepped in for her at meetings and called her by her first name.

She had always respected Luke's father. Always counted on him to be there when he was needed, and do what was right. Now, she was beginning to see him as a friend.

And on that note...

"Actually, Rae," he began hesitantly, "I was wondering if it would be alright if I stopped by the house later today? Checked in on Molly...?"

He's asking my permission? For a split second, Rae thought that 'first name' bit might have been strategic after all. But then the defenses lowered, and she acknowledged that wasn't true.

It had been Fodder who had carried Molly out of the factory the day of the fight. Luke was too far away, up in the sniper tower, to get to her as the dust began to settle. And she had broken a bone in her ankle, rendering her stranded on a high ledge with an excruciating limp.

Fodder had swooped in before she'd taken three steps.

He had watched her periodically throughout the battle. Whenever he had a free second, he found himself automatically scanning around for those people dearest to him. Much to his great surprise, he later admitted to Rae he found himself automatically including Molly in that list.

She was easy to spot, between the waves of neon lightning and the fiery wave of hair. But it was like Fodder hadn't really seen her until that day. Fighting tooth and nail for the people she loved. Risking everything she had to get them all one step closer. By the time he made it up to the ledge to reach her, he'd had to wade through a body count that was at least five high.

"Yeah, that sounds..." But Rae trailed off suddenly as she realized what a visit from the Commander might imply. "Actually, today's probably not the best. She's been super sick these past few mornings, and Luke won't leave her side. Maybe a raincheck?"

She felt horrible saying it. Any chance at 'family time' the three of them had to get to know each other was time well spent. But she couldn't exactly see that working with Simon Kerrigan locked in the basement just two stories below.

"Oh, of course." Fodder recovered himself quickly, looking embarrassed to have possibly overstepped. Rae's heart went out to him, but before she could say anything he looked up with a bright smile. "At any rate, I'll be over for your Thanksgiving."

Rae blinked. Then shook her head. Then blinked again.

"I'm sorry..." A fixed smile froze crookedly on her face. "Thanksgiving?"

"That's still on, isn't it?" he queried. "You seemed rather insistent with your invitation."

Insistent was understating it. Rae had been a holiday monster. Sure—it wasn't your typical English celebration, but it was one she'd been raised with in New York. Holidays were supposed to be fun. Were supposed to bring people together. To bask in each other's company while indulging themselves in entirely too much food. And while it certainly didn't feel as though they had much to be thankful for this year, looking at it from a different perspective they absolutely did.

They were alive, damn it. They had made it through. The only person no longer with them had given his life to ensure that they keep theirs. They were going to honor his sacrifice. They were going to live it out to the fullest. And they were going to set a place at the table for Carter.

"Yes, it's—it's definitely still on," Rae said quickly, trying to fight off a rising panic attack. "I just hadn't realized it was coming up so soon."

"The day after tomorrow," Fodder replied. "Fifteen-hundred hours?"

Rae fought the desire to roll her eyes. "Three o'clock. Yeah."

"Good." He nodded briskly. "I'm bringing pie."

He was off without another word, racing out of the parking lot at a speed that would have made Devon and Julian proud. It wasn't until he had already vanished around the shaded drive that Rae sucked in her first panicked gasp.

This can't be happening. This can't be happening

Then...

THIS IS HAPPENING!

Right on cue, her phone buzzed in her pocket. She picked it up without even looking, eyes still fixed on the place where Fodder had disappeared from view.

"Babe?"

Thank the Maker!

"Devon?! Listen, we've got a big problem—"

But far from calming her down, Devon was having problems of his own.

"Yeah, you could say that." He sounded nearly as distressed as she was. "Your mom just called. She wants to know who's picking her up from the airport."

Chapter 10

From a bird's eye view, Rae Kerrigan must have looked completely deranged. First freezing dead in place—hands still raised in the air in front of her. Then a blur of sudden speed, too fast to have possibly been human. Then coming to a standstill again, looking positively stunned.

Such was the way of things that morning. It was a series of starts and stops. Each more manic and disorienting than the last.

As slowly as Rae had driven out to Guilder, she made up for it now by racing back—flying through the countryside at a speed that would be considered most unwise now that she was no longer immortal. Lines of trees and the thatched roofs of little cottages became a picturesque blur, one that she hardly saw as she screeched into the driveway, sending up a spray of gravel in her wake.

"Devon?" she called as she streaked into the house. Her body had switched into Riley's cheetah tatù the second they'd hung up the phone, and she was having trouble slowing it down to move at an even remotely normal speed. She spotted a head of dark hair in the kitchen, and raced over, tossing her coat on the floor. "There you are! Listen, we're going to have to—"

She stopped cold the second she saw his face. Saw that careful smile that only barely disguised the traces of utter panic beneath.

"Look who's up!" he said pointedly, gesturing over his shoulder with a strained grin.

Rae took a split second to shift gears, then looked behind him to realize that the little kitchen was filled to the brim. Filled with smiling faces. One face stood out in particular.

"Molly!"

The tiny redhead stepped forward, looking better than she had in days. One hand was clutched firmly in Luke's, while the other held onto a steaming mug of tea like it was a life raft. Rae could smell the ginger all the way across the room.

"In the flesh!" Molly beamed, still weak but smiling. "You think this is impressive—I was able to eat an entire saltine right before you got here. Happened right over there."

She pointed over to the kitchen table with a look of great importance, and despite the massive storm cloud hovering just overhead Rae couldn't help but chuckle as she moved forward to give her best friend a gentle hug. For the first time in ages, she didn't feel like it might break Molly to do so. There was a hint of color in her pale cheeks. A delicate shade of pink that seemed to get stronger the more she drank.

Well, that explains it...

The hopeful vibe. The smiling faces. The Norman Rockwell impersonation.

Quite the contrast from where they were yesterday afternoon. It seemed that everyone had needed to take a step back from the 'Simon Kerrigan' fiasco as much as she did. And Molly's recovery was the perfect reason to do it.

"I'm so glad you're feeling better!" Rae gripped her as tight as she dared, before pulling back to flash Luke a warm smile as well. "You look like you're feeling better, too."

That was understating it.

It was like he'd gone through some sort of magical transformation. Gone were the dark hollows beneath his eyes and cheekbones. Vanished was the blind, unadulterated panic that had perpetually dilated his eyes. When she'd raced into the bathroom the previous day to find Molly lying on the floor, Rae literally thought they might have to give Luke some sort of sedative as well.

But now...?

It looked like a flame had been lit inside him, illuminating him from the inside out. His eyes sparkled as they stared down at the top of Molly's head, and even when she and Rae had tried to lean in for an embrace he wouldn't let go of her hand. He held on awkwardly instead, pulling her right back into his chest the second they were done.

"Oh, I know." Molly lowered her voice conspiratorially, "Didn't he look awful? I mean, I feel like it's the elephant in the room—maybe we should just get it over with and talk about it."

That was the elephant? Not that Simon Kerrigan was tied up in the basement?

Yep, they needed a break alright.

And if the Privy Council had taught Rae anything, it was how to compartmentalize...

She flashed Luke an incredulous look, but he simply closed his eyes with a long-suffering grin. "Honey, I told you, I had more important things on my mind than to deep condition."

The rest of the room snickered quietly, but Molly had never been more serious. "Sweetheart, I know it's uncomfortable, but we *have* to talk about it. Friends hold friends accountable. Here, I'll even go first." She looked encouragingly around the room, as if staging some sort of misguided intervention. "I think you honestly looked better when you were in a coma."

Classic Molly.

She turned with a gracious smile to Julian, hoping to pass the torch, but he wasn't having it. Instead, he swooped down without the slightest bit of warning and kissed her on the cheek.

"We missed you, Molls." He stepped back with a grin, ruffling her wavy hair. A bolt of lightning was quick to follow.

Yep...she's back.

"Breakfast?" he queried, stepping strategically behind Devon to avoid her wrath. It was only then that Rae realized there was something burning on the stove. "My treat."

Despite the sad state of whatever was supposed to be cooking in the pan, Rae nodded with an overabundance of enthusiasm and helped herself to some coffee. If she had come here to deliver yet another bombshell, perhaps it was best they didn't hear it on an empty stomach. Not to mention, it would give her more time to come up with some sort of plan.

"Absolutely!" She took her first sip, staring curiously at the stove. "Uh...what is it?"

Julian beamed with pride. "Pancakes."

A spray of coffee flew through her nose.

Pancakes. It had to be pancakes.

The room turned to stare at her in slow motion as she grabbed a napkin, dabbing furiously at her face. "Actually, uh...I think I'm good on breakfast."

"Really?" Julian looked hurt. "You love pancakes."

"Jules," Molly said gently, "that looks like something died."

He prodded at it hopefully with the spatula, but when pieces of it actually splintered away, he flipped off the burner with a sigh. "It looked so easy online..."

"You didn't use any butter," Luke explained, coming over to investigate. The two of them peered down into the smoking pan like scientists observing an experiment gone awry. "You need some sort of oil on there, otherwise it will stick to the pan."

"How do you possibly know that?" Molly piped up, coming to stand between them. "The last thing you tried to 'cook' for me was soup, and you managed to break our microwave."

Luke avoided her eyes and flushed defensively. "After which time, I began reading up on it."

Rae watched their every move, growing more and more depressed by the second.

They were trying. Trying *so hard* to act like they were getting better. Trying so hard to act like everything was going back to normal, despite the lunatic she'd stashed in the basement. And now, she was about to pull the rug out from under them once again.

Across the kitchen, Devon nodded encouragingly and tapped his watch. The time for stall tactics had passed. They were on a deadline.

Right. No problem. Just ease into it.

"Hey, guys...?" she began tentatively.

"Maybe there's still a chance of resurrecting it," Julian said hopefully. "What if we added some flour? You know, to lighten it up a little?"

Molly seized upon this idea enthusiastically, but Luke shook his head.

"And then what? Hold a séance? No, we need to start from the beginning."

"Guys?"

"You know what you should do, Julian, is get drunk," Molly said practically. "You know how whiskey steadies your hands. That's why Devon's stitches turned out so well."

Julian rubbed his chin. "That's true. I'm not sure what we have here, but—"

"It's ten in the morning!" Luke cried in exasperation. "No! It is possible to make pancakes while sober. Trust me. We just need to—"

"THE   DAY   AFTER   TOMORROW   IS THANKSGIVING!"

Not exactly easing in, but it got the message across...

The three of them slowly turned back around, blinking with matching expressions of shock as the stove smoked steadily behind them. Whether they were making the connection with Simon or they simply thought she was having a festive meltdown was unclear.

Finally, after a long silence, it was Julian who spoke.

"Well that's...ironic."

Plans were set aside for later, the fire on the stove was put out, and reinforcements were called in. Both Gabriel and Angel had been conspicuously absent the entire morning, but after numerous tries Julian was finally able to get a hold of Angel on her cell.

"Are they coming?" Rae asked as he joined the rest of them in the parlor.

They had set up a makeshift command station in the center of the room, pulling their chairs around in a tight circle. It was a method they had used many times before when gearing up for a battle. One way or another, the looming holiday wasn't shaping up to be much different.

"Yeah, they're on their way." He took a seat beside Devon with a little frown. "She sounded weird, though. Off...somehow. I couldn't hear well enough to figure out why."

"Maybe it's because she knows the sky is about to come crashing down on our heads." Molly smiled sweetly. The faster the ginger worked its way through her system, perking up her deadened nerve endings, the faster she'd deflected the blame for their present situation with the force of a nova. "I still maintain that if I hadn't been holed up in the bathroom, trying to grow this little monster, none of this would have happened."

"Yeah, yeah, we know." Devon rubbed his temples. "You're the voice of reason."

"Damn right, Wardell. And I'd watch that tone if I were you. Unless you want me to call off your wedding."

He rolled his eyes dismissively, but the longer she stared at him the more nervous he seemed to become. Finally, he shifted casually in his seat towards Rae. His obviously restless fiancée. "Can she really do that?"

"Haven't you heard," Rae kept her eyes on the door, "it's Molly's wedding. We're just the ones who happen to be getting married."

The boys laughed softly before trailing off into nervous silence. Molly was the only one who didn't seem to think it was a joke, but she, too, kept her eyes on the clock. It wasn't until they heard the rev of an engine, followed by the telltale crunch of gravel under boots, that they managed to really breathe for the first time.

Gabriel and Angel would know what to do.

It was an unspoken assumption. One that every person seated in the ring of chairs realized they had come to rely upon more than they realized. Whenever things got too twisted, whenever the ethical compass was buried so far in the mud they couldn't see which way to go, they turned to their resident sociopaths to point them in the right direction.

For better or worse, the adopted siblings had been raised beneath a cemetery by an evil mastermind. They'd been to hell and back. Had braved death, torture, and what could only be described as a routine 'loss of soul,' since they were first toddling around the catacombs. Whatever the assignment, the sacrifice, the trial.... they could handle it.

Surely they could handle Thanksgiving as well.

Then the lyrics of a long-forgotten Phil Collins song drifted in from the porch. Sung in the lilting voices of a high soprano, and a booming bass.

"Cause you'll be in my heart! You'll BE IN my heart!"

The voices choked off in laugher, gasping and reprimanding each other before having at it once more. Rae and the others locked eyes across the room.

"From this day on! Now and forever—NO! Gabriel! That's where the monkey grabs him!"

Rae sank down in her chair and covered her face with her hands.

Correction: if there was one thing *Cromfield* taught you, it was how to compartmentalize.

The door burst open and brother and sister stumbled inside. They were clinging to each other for balance. Skin flushed, and eyes over-bright with intoxication. A virtual cloud of whiskey and vodka followed them in, and not only were they completely oblivious to the somber atmosphere but they seemed constantly on the verge of laughing.

"Sweetie?" Julian said tentatively, rising to his feet. "Are you—"

"JULES!"

The second she saw him, Angel flung her body carelessly through the air. Unfortunately, she was equally oblivious to the glass coffee table that lay in between them.

"*Whoa!* I got you." He literally snatched her out of the air at the last second, cradling her against his chest as she gazed up at him with those hypnotic sapphire eyes. The eyes momentarily derailed him, and his lips curved up in a tender smile. "Hey there," he brushed strands of long white hair out of her face. "Did someone discover the local pub?"

"Jules, we planted a flag."

Both siblings burst out laughing once again, and Gabriel half-fell into the chair next to Rae, seemingly unable to stay standing for a moment longer. "Seriously, man, thanks for that!"

Julian's smile froze on his face. "Thanks? What do you..." He trailed off with an air of resignation as Angel fished his credit card out of her pocket and slapped it back into his hand. "Oh. Right."

"I found it when I was pilfering your wallet," she shrugged innocently. "Honest mistake."

Devon bit his lip and stared at the ground, while Julian took a steadying breath.

"Well, that's...great, honey. I'm glad you two had some fun."

"SO much fun!" she exclaimed. "They gave us a lifetime ban!"

"They banned you?" Julian repeated incredulously. "What for?"

Her face lit up with excitement. "Well, it's actually—"

"—it's actually a really uninteresting story you promised to take to your grave," Gabriel interjected smoothly, flashing his sister a threatening grin. His golden hair spilled messily into his eyes as he tilted his head back against the chair. "And don't worry about the card, Decker. We only used it for absolute emergencies."

Angel nodded seriously. "Like bail."

"Wait...WHAT?!"

"Not important now, buddy." Devon clapped him sympathetically on the shoulder, pushing him back into his chair at the same time. "We called you guys because we actually have a serious problem. And we're trying to figure out what to do."

He turned to Rae, who took over with a nervous nod.

"The day after tomorrow is Thanksgiving."

Gabriel and Angel stared at her with twin expressions. Both coming up blank. Finally, after a moment's pause, a flicker of recognition flashed across Angel's face.

"Like...the holiday?"

Molly shook her head sanctimoniously. "...left in the cave too long..."

"Yes, like the holiday," Rae snapped, bringing them back on point. She turned to Gabriel with an accusatory stare. "I told you about this a week ago. I sent an invitation to your flat."

"You mailed me a card you printed out at four in the morning with a turkey on it," Gabriel said without an ounce of humor. "I thought it was a joke."

Rae crossed her arms over her chest, feeling defensive. "How would that have been a joke?"

"I didn't say I thought it was a very *good* joke."

"How is it that you never fail to be absolutely infur—"

"The point is," Devon intervened once again, "Rae invited her mother and Luke's father to celebrate. They'll be here the day after tomorrow."

Angel shrugged, the vodka haze clouding his implication. "Okay, well, we'll be on our best behavior. Won't blow anything up, or act remotely like ourselves." She sat up a bit straighter, tossing back her sheet of iridescent hair with a touch of impatience. "And for the record, you guys don't have to give us this speech every time—"

"They're coming *here*," Gabriel interrupted, catching on. "To the house?"

Rae nodded, fighting back the automatic wave of panic.

His eyes clouded as he exchanged a quick look with Angel.

"Wait, you said your mom? The day after tomorrow—"

"Yes," Rae interrupted, "which means we have a few options. We can gag my father and barricade the door so that no one goes down there. We can have Angel freeze him, although that would mean she'd have to touch his skin."

"Hang on," Gabriel held up his hand, "Rae—"

"We can bring him back out to the boathouse—although there's a risk that people will want to park their cars out there. Not that I know how my mom is getting from here to the airport yet."

"Seriously, Rae, wait—"

"Come to think of it, I don't even know when her flight is coming in."

"RAE!"

"WHAT, Gabriel?!" she shouted, the panic finally spilling over. "I don't have time to wait! I just found out that my father is actually ALIVE, I'm keeping him tied up in my BASEMENT, and my freakin' MOTHER is going to land on English soil at any moment! So, WHAT IS IT?!"

There was a strangled gasp and Rae's eyes jumped immediately to the front door.

Beth slumped against the doorway, her silver purse slipping from her hands. Rae stared in horror as Gabriel turned white as a sheet.

"I was going to tell you who gave us a ride home..."

Chapter 11

Everything happened a lot faster after Gabriel spoke—before Rae could stop them.

For half a second her mother slumped against the doorway, looking for all the world like she was about to faint. The second after, she was a towering column of ice blue flames tearing through the mansion like a lioness on the prowl.

As Rae stared after her, palsied with momentary shock, a random memory flashed through her mind: the day she had gone in to the relator's office to sign the papers for the house. The fact that, as if wishing could make it so, she had neglected to purchase the renter's insurance that came with it. Two little words floated to the surface of her mind. Fire damage.

Then there was a scream from the lower hallway, and the words were replaced by two others.

Simon Kerrigan.

Then the war room sprang into action—tearing after her, Rae and her cheetah tatù leading the way. Only Gabriel and Angel stayed behind. One, feeling too guilty at having been too drunk to speak up earlier. The other, passed out on the couch.

It was the strangest game of 'follow the breadcrumbs' Rae had ever played. Instead of tracking down little notes or trails of ribbons, she and her friends followed the heat. The scorching, unrelenting heat of her mother's rage, manifested into the glowing flames that clung to her.

She had just reached the door to the basement when they caught up with her. By this point, even her hair was burning with flames. It had begun to float around her like a fiery cloud, scorching all it touched.

"Mom!" Rae called, skidding to a stop on the wooden floor. She took a halting step forward, then stopped again, her face crumbling in misery. "Mom, I'm so sorry. I'm *so sorry* I didn't tell you."

Beth ignored her.

Clearly focusing only on the problem at hand. And by the looks of things, it was a problem she intended to fix on the spot.

"He's down there? Tied up?"

The questions fired out like bullets, each more deadly than the last.

"We found him in the cells beneath the old factory." Rae's voice dropped to a guilty whisper, trying to get out as many facts as she could. Every second she reasoned with her mother was another second she kept her father alive. "Devon, me, and a contingent of guards. At first, none of us believed it. Everyone—the world was so certain he was dead..."

"As he should be," Beth snapped.

The flames curling around her showed no signs of abating. Quite the contrary, the longer she stood there the hotter they seemed to burn. It got to the point where the gang had to start squinting just to keep her in focus, hands raised to shield their eyes as they winced against the heat.

Rae alone stepped forward, angling between the fire and the door. It was the last place in the world she wanted to be, but was the only one who could stand and not get burned.

"Cromfield took him prisoner," she continued in the same, soft monotone. "Locked him in a cell for almost fifteen years. I only—"

"Then for almost fifteen years we were safe," Beth spat. "For almost fifteen years, the world got the rest and peace it deserved after having endured a man like Simon Kerrigan. You say it like it's so much time, Rae. It doesn't even begin to scratch the surface! He deserves lifetimes of imprisonment. A life sentence for every life he stole." Her face twisted with bitterness. "And I don't just mean the people he murdered; I'm talking about the other lives as well. The ones he broke, the ones he buried and stole. The ones he ruined beyond repair."

The world around Rae swam as she stared at the flames through eyes full of tears. Behind her, the others were frozen in similar states of shock. Suddenly, despite all their talent and years of experience, they looked very much their young age.

Only Gabriel, who had caught up with them by now, was staring at Beth like he got her. Like she alone was the only one making sense of this whole thing. Like she knew exactly the correct reaction to Simon Kerrigan being alive.

"Then there are people who'd say that mere imprisonment isn't enough." Beth's own voice was dangerously quiet, sending chills up her daughter's spine. "That Simon deserves to die for what he did. That the world would be a better place. That everyone in it... would be safer." Her eyes rested on Rae for a briefest of moments, before hardening ice blue. "And I'm one of them."

Rae stared, shocked and unable to respond.

Beth reached for the door without another second's pause, ready to finish what a fire had started all those years ago. Ready to end the infamous legacy of Simon Kerrigan once and for all.

Rae shifted to move to block her mother. Another memory raced through Rae's mind. She had seen something like this before. In the old kitchen, at her old house, almost fifteen years ago.

When Simon came home that day, he had been in a rage. He'd just found out that his own wife had been working for the Privy Council against him, and he was determined, one way or another, to escalate things to their violent end.

He'd tried everything he could to bait her. Threats, screams, insults. Nothing worked. Beth kept her cool, kept her head.

Angry, but controlling it. Even then, at the bitter end, fighting *for* the things she loved—not *against* them.

It wasn't until he mentioned Rae that all of that changed.

Rae remembered it like it had happened yesterday. Like peering through a looking glass, a crystal-clear image shimmered before her eyes.

Beth had turned on a dime. The second she heard her daughter's name.

One minute, she was a frustrated wife. Aggressive, but defensive. Not willing to take things to that next step. Then in that next minute? She was an enraged mother. Protective beyond belief. Enraged beyond belief. Willing to go to the next step and beyond if it meant keeping her daughter safe.

It was those protective instincts that Rae needed to call upon now. As counter-intuitive as it seemed, perhaps there was a way out of this that didn't end in bloodshed.

"I can't see that again." Her voice broke halfway through, shuddering even as she tried to keep it strong. "I've seen this fight before, Mom. I can't go through it again."

No. She couldn't watch her parents battle each other once more. She couldn't watch the two of them fight to the bitter end.

But even more than that, she couldn't let her mother go through that either. Beth had already buried this husband. Already lost enough of herself in the process. Rae couldn't stand by now and let her kill the first man she'd ever loved.

Simon Kerrigan had taken enough from her. Rae wasn't going to let him take that, too.

For the first time since stepping into the house, Beth's face softened. Only fractionally. Hardly enough to be encouraging. Her hands lowered just half an inch, and the ice blue flames whipping around her began to lighten back to white around the edges.

"Sweetheart," she spoke with strained patience, "it's *not safe* for him to be here. It isn't safe for him to be anywhere, let alone in the same house as you. I simply won't allow it." Her eyes flickered briefly over to Devon before narrowing with a silent accusation. "I'm surprised it was allowed at all."

He bowed his head to his chest, staring depressingly at the floor.

"Now, whether you see it is entirely up to you. You can go up to your room, you can stand there by the door. But one way or another, Simon Kerrigan is not leaving this place alive."

A cascade of shivers ran down Rae's arms, but she held firm. "Do you hear yourself?" she asked incredulously. "You're 'sending me up to my room' so that you can murder my dad! This isn't okay—"

"He's not your *DAD*!"

The word echoed through the hallway, coming back louder and louder every time.

Rae paused a moment. Stunning. *Not my dad?* Impossible. The mark on her back, her ability—

Beth cut off her train of thought as she glared at the basement door and then back to Rae. "A dad is a man who loves you. Who takes care of you. Who pretends to like your terrible artwork and takes you to dance class on the weekends. Your dad is a man who's always there for you. Who puts himself second, so that he can put you first. A man who would never, *ever* do anything that could cause you pain. Or harm you." Beth's face twisted with the blackest kind of rage. "Simon Kerrigan is not that man."

There was a muffled gasp from several feet below, and Rae felt suddenly sure that Simon himself had heard them. How could he not? The love of his life was screaming from the top the stairs.

"He's not capable of that kind of love," Beth continued, her voice both hard and somehow gentle at the same time. "He's not capable of love at all."

She was right. *Was* she right? At this point, did it matter?

Rae's head was spinning with so many questions, her body was heavy with so many emotions, she felt like she couldn't stand for a second more. There was a faint rustling sound, and the next second Devon was standing tall behind her, holding her discreetly against his chest.

"Beth," he said quietly, "no one here is disputing that. Not a word of it. You're *absolutely* right about every single part. We're just saying—"

"Andrew would be ashamed."

The words cracked like a whip between them and Devon pulled in a quick breath, flinching as if they caused him actual pain.

"He worked his whole life trying to keep Rae safe. Trying to protect her from the continuing ripple-effect of what that man had done. The continuing horrors he inflicted. And now you invited this abomination of a man himself into your house. Into *Rae's* house."

For one of the first times in his life, Devon seemed completely unable to speak. He just stood there, his face shadowed with a look of heartbreaking sadness.

"Mrs. C," Julian began gently, trying his best to intercede for his friend, "he was just trying to say that, whatever Simon's guilty of, the punishment shouldn't be—"

"And you." Beth's eyes cooled as they fell upon yet another boy she thought of as a surrogate son. "You didn't *see* this coming? Or are you not doing that anymore?"

He flinched back, stung, and fell quiet.

Molly didn't know what to say either, and Luke didn't seem to feel it was his place.

In the end, it was only Gabriel who was left to speak.

Rae watched as he stared first at his incapacitated friends—each one of them reduced to nothing by just a few choice words said by exactly the right person. Crippled by guilt. Crippled by doubt. Crippled by the dark belief that maybe Beth was right. Maybe a murderer's life should end today.

Then he turned his eyes to Rae standing in the middle of it all.

Despite all her strength he believed she had, he had clearly never seen her so lost. Never seen her so utterly gutted by the scene in front of her. She'd seen one father die. She'd grown up believing her mother was dead as well. Her grandparents had been murdered. She'd lost friends, mentors, people she was supposed to have been able to trust. Just weeks ago, she'd put on a black dress and lowered into the ground the one person who had been like a parent to her since coming to Guilder.

And now... she was about to go through all of it again.

His muscles tensed in protest, and Rae could almost see the internal battle waging behind those lovely eyes. The desire to protect warring with the desire to kill. The purest kind of love against the darkest kind of revenge.

Then, with a silent breath, he turned his eyes to Beth.

"You can't kill him."

It was simple and direct. No mincing of words, no leniency in their offer. All in all, it was a very *Gabriel* way of ending the conversation.

"No one in the world has more reason to hate him," he said softly. "No one in the world has more reason to see him gone... Except maybe me."

The room went quiet.

No one dared take a breath. No one dared to even move for fear that the entire house of cards would come crashing down in flames.

Except... those flames were cooling now. Growing gentler and gentler the longer Beth stared into Gabriel's eyes.

"Julian was right," he continued quietly. "No matter what Simon is guilty of, the punishment shouldn't be revenge. It should be law. No one here is saying he gets away scot-free." He took a careful step forward, placing himself on Rae's other side. "Simon broke the law. And he will be punished for that. He broke people, too...but we don't give ourselves over to revenge."

He lifted his head and looked Rae right in the eye. "We don't do that."

It was one of those moments Rae knew she would remember forever. The kind that went on to define people. That went on to shape the things that would come. A *coming of age* is what Carter would have called it.

For a second, just a second, she saw a glimmer of what Gabriel could have been if he had never been brought down into those caves. For a split second, she saw a different version of him.

Untainted, unbroken. A boy laughing in the sun, bright and free.

Maybe there was a chance for that guy after all.

Rae hoped beyond anything that there was. Her heart clenched in her chest as she wished she could make that happen. All the tatùs in the world couldn't help her. They couldn't change the past.

At long last, Beth slowly lowered her hands. The flames around her vanished into thin air, but somehow the woman left standing was in no way diminished. In fact, she looked even taller. "You said you found him in the factory?" She kept her eyes on the door, but directed the question to her daughter. "He'd been there all this time?"

Rae nodded in a daze, unable to believe what had just happened.

"And no one else knows he's here? Just the guards who were with you?"

"Guards who have been sworn to secrecy," Rae added swiftly. "I trust them."

Beth's eyes flickered to her for a split second, then returned to the door. "Why didn't you just arrest him? Have the guards take him away to await trial?"

This was where it got dicey. This was where the whole thing had started to unravel, and this whole game of 'hide the Kerrigan' had begun.

"I knocked him out," she confessed, remembering that part of it for the first time. "He was lying on the ground, and the next thing I knew a dozen guns were pointed at his head. Mitch Ford—you remember our new head of security? He wanted to shoot him right there. Seemed to think it was the practical thing to do." She sucked in a shuddering breath. "He asked my permission..."

Then all at once she was in Beth's arms. There are few things stronger than a mother's love and, even with the man who had single-handedly demolished her life sitting just a stone's throw away, Beth couldn't stand to see her daughter hurting.

She held her for a long time, one hand clasped on the back of her head as the other wrapped tightly around her back. They rocked back and forth, oblivious to how much time had passed, or to the others who were still standing there. Taking comfort only in their little family. The two women who had, against all the odds, managed to remain.

"You did the right thing," she finally whispered, lips pressed against Rae's dark hair. "You did the right thing."

A gut-wrenching sob tore its way through Rae's body and she pressed her face into her mother's shoulder, every inch of her body vibrating with the relief of hearing those words. "Do you really think so?" she whispered. "You're not just saying that? Because, Mom, I don't know what I'm supposed to do—"

Beth pulled back, gripping her firmly by the shoulders and cutting off her words. "You had a choice. Either to kill a man in cold blood...or not to. You chose not. As your mother, how can I be anything but proud of that choice?" She looked briefly around the room, resting on each of the circle of friends. "A choice that all of you supported. Making it a choice you all made yourselves." Her eyes twinkled as they rested on each one, coming to stop on Gabriel. "It's no less than what I expect from you."

Then she circled back once more to the door. That lovely twinkle vanished on the spot, replaced with a kind of weary endurance that Rae had seen before.

Rae wished she knew what to say. Wished she knew how to be more like... more like... her mother.

"Our problem, however, remains." Beth pressed her jaw tight.

Yes, it most certainly did. And despite the attempted homicide, despite the trail of smoke stains leading from the foyer to the door to the basement, Rae couldn't have been more relieved to have her mother standing by her side.

No matter what came next, they would face it together.

Mother and daughter. Standing side by side.

"Do you want to talk to him?" Rae asked quietly, wondering rather morbidly at how that conversation would play out.

Beth considered for a moment, her lips thinning into a hard line, before she shook her head. "No. I want to think first. Work out some kind of plan of action, before I actually go down there and look at that face." A faint shudder rippled through her, and for a split second Rae was the one ready to throw protective flames. "He's tied up securely, with tatù-inhibitors in place?" she asked Devon. "You did it yourself?"

"Yes, ma'am," he answered quietly, eyes still on the floor.

Despite her later revelation, he obviously couldn't get over her first stabbing words. They had cut to the core of him, and whether he'd earned tentative forgiveness or not, Rae knew that Devon was probably—he couldn't help—wondering if she was right.

Beth's face softened as she looked him over. "Devon?" He lifted his eyes slowly, struggling to meet hers. "It's still Beth, okay?"

His body relaxed the slightest degree, and he flashed her a hint of a smile. "Okay."

She smiled warmly, then gestured up the hall. "Fine. Now everyone back to the parlor. We have a plan to come up with, and a holiday dinner to save..."

And just like that, it was over.

The gang dispersed, following Beth back to the main house. She grabbed Julian on the way over, kissing him on the forehead in apology, then wiping away the lipstick with a motherly thumb.

In the end, it was only Rae and Gabriel left standing by the basement door.

His chest rose and fell quickly as he stared at the door. Whether he completely believed everything he'd said earlier—it was hard to say. The only obvious thing was that it was apparently killing him to simply walk away.

"Hey," Rae slipped her hand into his own, giving it a tight squeeze, "you okay?"

He glanced down at her with a truly unreadable expression, then back up at the door. "Yeah. Sure."

Despite all his attempts at bravado, he still swayed slightly where he stood. You couldn't undo the evils of so much alcohol through strength of will alone, and Rae helped to steady him with a little smile.

"You know, all that stuff you said? I'm just happy you didn't slur."

His lips curved up in a grin that didn't meet his eyes. They were still busy with the door. "Me, too. Probably would've taken something away from the delivery."

Rae laughed softly, but looked back up at him with a truly tender expression. "Does it sound patronizing if I say... I'm really proud of you?"

There was a slightly awkward pause as both considered it at the same time.

"Yeah," Gabriel finally replied. "It does."

But he looked up with just a hint of that old sparkle.

"Don't be proud, Rae. I wasn't inventing—I was repeating." A flash of that same tenderness gentled him as well. "It was a lesson I learned from you."

Chapter 12

"You want to tell my dad?"

For the second time on the same day, the group had retreated to their makeshift war room, gathering around in a circle of chairs. Only this time, there were a few minor changes.

Beth was seated between Rae and Devon. A hand placed on each of their legs, her body constantly angled towards the door, as if at any moment her not-dead husband might spring forth and wreak havoc on all of them.

Angel lay on the couch, still passed out cold on the couch, snoring loudly. At one point, Julian had tried to wake her. But she had rolled over in her sleep and slapped him across the face so hard he seemed reluctant to try it again.

Gabriel also had a chair in the circle, although he seemed in constant danger of going the way of his sister. He was seated by Molly, of all people, and every time he threatened to doze off a tiny surge of electricity shot discreetly into his side.

But it was Luke who had the spotlight. However unwanted it might be.

His chair had been nudged coaxingly to the center of the ring as the others angled discreetly around it. It had been almost too subtle at first to notice, but now that the meeting had started the intention was too obvious to miss.

"Me. My dad." He looked desperately from face to face as the walls started to close in. "You want me to call my dad right now, and tell him that Simon Kerrigan is tied up in our basement?"

The decision to tell Mr. Fodder was universal, as it seemed to be the natural solution to all their problems. It had been the first thing out of Beth's mouth the second they walked back into the living room, but everyone was quick to claim the idea as their own.

Everyone except Luke.

"Don't be silly," Gabriel shook his head, still caught in the after-effects of his whiskey-induced haze, "we don't want you to call him. We want you to wait until he comes for Thanksgiving dinner. Then tell him."

A look of true panic flickered across Luke's face, and Rae was quick to intervene.

"He's going to know what to do with this," she said deliberately, hoping that her newfound calm might be catching. "I can't possibly be expected to make this kind of decision myself, not when it comes to members of my own family. But your dad? He's the most level-headed, experienced man I've ever met. He'll know what to do."

Molly leaned forward sympathetically, hand resting lightly atop her flat stomach.

"He might even be grateful to you, babe. That you trust him enough to confide this big a secret. That you're surrendering the responsibility into his hands."

Luke slid his fingers up into his wilted mohawk, giving him an even slightly more manic air. "Yeah, *or* he's going to say, 'Luke, what the hell were you possibly thinking?!'" His voice lowered into such a frightfully accurate impression that, for a second, all of them got chills. "Did any of you stop to think that this is going to look an *awful* lot like that time I failed to tell him Cromfield had returned? You know... *that* tiny omission?"

That I did for all of YOU.

The silent implication was clear.

Luke had been sticking his neck out for longer than Rae could even remember. Making sacrifice after sacrifice just to protect the people he loved. To find a way to keep them in his life.

On the one hand, his allegiance with the Knights had kind of demanded it. If he was going to toe the line between the two worlds, it made sense that he would be forced to make certain allowances along the way. But the rest was just Luke.

He was a good man. One of the best people Rae had ever met, hands down. Even now, fidgeting beneath an uncomfortable spotlight, she knew he would do the right thing.

Rae swallowed, determined to convince him. "Yeah, but this way, right after you tell him you can hand him a gigantic piece of pie." She nudged him playfully, hoping to coax a smile. "Crisis averted."

He sighed miserably and sank an inch or two lower in his chair. But even with the prospect of the confession looming in front of him, it was impossible not to see the wisdom in the plan.

For better or worse, Anthony Fodder was a man who could be trusted. Furthermore, he was perhaps the only man in the world who could ensure Simon Kerrigan's protection until the day of his trial. The Abbey, where he was still located, wasn't set up like the PC holding cells. It granted access to one person, and one person only. Commander Fodder himself. As long as Simon was under his protection, he would be safe.

Finally, when the silence could go on no longer, Luke lifted his head. "Do you at least promise that you won't conjure it? This has to be a homemade... well at least, store-bought pie, okay?"

Molly jumped forward to wrap her arms around his neck, while Rae and the boys shot each other looks of deep relief.

Beth, on the other hand, was all business. "Right." She stood up, clasping her hands. "In that case, we've got to make this as seamless a transition as we possibly can. What were you all planning on serving for dinner?"

"Pizza."

The ringing answer came from every corner of the room. Even Angel lifted her head off the couch to chime in, before passing out once more.

Beth raised her eyebrows carefully, staring them all down in turn. "... Pizza?"

It *did* sound a bit childish. Especially the longer she allowed it to hang in the air. Rae gulped and shot Devon a quick look. "Or...we could always do a more traditional version of the meal? You know, turkey, and yams, and potatoes, and such."

"Seriously?" Devon dropped his voice to half-volume to speak only to her. "You want the seven of us to cook a Thanksgiving dinner with your dad tied up downstairs? You want the seven of us to try to cook a Thanksgiving dinner—period?"

She shrugged, suddenly trying not to grin. "We've done stranger things."

"And how's Molly supposed to deal with all those smells?"

"Actually," Molly said as she perched upon Luke's lap, "that all sounds incredible."

That alone was enough to get Luke on board. Julian was soon to follow, and after a pointed look from Beth Devon hopped on bandwagon as well.

In the end, all that was left to do was the logistics.

Beth stood. "Right, well, we've got just a day to pull this off." She began pacing back and forth in front of them like a general. You could take a girl out of the Privy Council, but you could never quite remove that unshakable Privy Council discipline from the girl. "Anthony Fodder will be here first thing in the morning to visit, before we all sit down at noon. That means we'll need to pick up ingredients and get the house ready this afternoon, if we want to start baking by the evening."

Baking by the evening? Exactly how elaborate was this dinner supposed to be?

Apparently, the boys were thinking the same thing.

Julian shot Devon a rather startled expression at the prospect of being trapped in the kitchen, to which Devon nodded quickly and leaned forward with his best diplomatic smile. Rae watched from the corner, not missing anything but determined not to say anything until she had to.

"Beth," Devon said as he forced his smile to stay friendly, "I'm not sure there's really that much to be done. I mean... get the house ready? I don't know what all you're talking about, but—"

"There's a half-burnt mannequin and a flame thrower on the front porch."

That settled it.

The rest of the morning was spent in a flurry of hasty preparation, most of which involved dousing the mansion in enough sanitizing chemicals to clean a small country.

The windows had to be opened to air the whole thing out, the floors scrubbed until the marble began to shine, and all the boys took turns arguing over who got to ride the enormous lawnmower they'd discovered in the back of the gardener's shed.

Rae watched them with a smile from the window, up to her elbows in a sink full of soapy suds. The house had all the modern amenities you'd expect for the hefty price they'd paid, except for one minor detail. A dishwasher. It was a testament to how un-domesticated the gang had become, that none of them noticed this fact until Beth pointed it out.

"... Give a bunch of kids a two-million-euro mansion, and they want to fill it with pizza..."

Rae glanced over her shoulder with a grin as Beth joined her at the sink. One washed, and one dried. An efficient assembly line they did in comfortable silence as they gazed out the window.

The argument over the mower had progressed beyond the constructs of the natural world. They were using powers now. And they weren't holding back their punches.

"You know," Rae murmured thoughtfully, "as crazy as it sounds...that's about the most normal I've seen them. Right there."

Beth followed her gaze to where Gabriel was summoning the machine towards himself from across the lawn, Luke chasing him with the flame thrower.

"Boys will be boys. That's pretty much the same across the board." She chuckled as Julian's shirt caught on fire, and began wiping down a plate. "You know, there's something important I neglected to ask you. A question that should've been the first one out of my mouth." She set down the plate, and gestured for Rae to do the same. "How are you doing, honey?"

How am I doing? That's a tough one...

Rae slowly lifted her hands out of the sudsy water as she contemplated where she should even begin. There were so many emotions battling for dominance, it was hard to pick just one of them. In the end, it wasn't even up to her. The word just popped out of her mouth.

"Relieved."

She didn't mean to say it. Odds were, she should've kept it to herself. But the fact of the matter remained. Despite the chaos simmering just below the surface, the insurmountable problem sitting just a dozen or so feet below...the feeling reigned supreme.

"I'm sorry, Mom," she apologized quickly. "That's probably the very *last* thing you want to hear right now—"

"No, not at all." Beth lay a soothing hand on her arm. "Explain. Talk to me."

Rae pulled in a deep breath, trying to string enough coherent thoughts together that they would possibly make sense. "I'm relieved that we're all here today."

She glanced outside the window to see that Molly had wandered out to the deck with a bowls of popcorn to watch the epic fight. Angel was now passed out cold on the tire swing, slumped over and drooling, and the flame thrower was now the least of the artillery on the field.

"I'm relieved that, after everything we just went through, we're all still standing. We're all still here to throw this ridiculous dinner idea. We're living in this house. We're trying to...to mend."

There was a series of screams as Gabriel fell to the grass in a splash of blood.

"Even if we're going about it in rather unconventional ways."

She hazarded a glance at her mother's face, but Beth didn't seem the least bit put off by anything she was saying. Quite the contrary, despite the gaping hole in her own life, she looked as though she whole-heartedly agreed.

"You're here with me," Rae continued, taking her by the hand with a smile. "Despite all the odds, all the impossible things that were stacked against us—we're both still standing here. Washing dishes just like none of it ever happened." Then she looked down at their hands, and her smile faded. "...and my father's not dead."

Beth's fingers stiffened, but she didn't pull away. Her eyes watered, but she didn't cry. She simply bowed her head to her chest with a quiet sigh.

"Mom, I can't be happy about that. I can't be happy that he's alive." Rae hesitated, trying to frame it the correct way. "But I couldn't be happy he was dead, either. The only thing I can really feel is... relieved."

There was a long pause. Filled only with the occasional scream from outside.

Rae hesitated and then asked her mother a question softly, "Does that make me a terrible person?"

"No, sweetie. Of course not." Beth gathered her into her arms, ignoring the soap suds that came between them. "It isn't human to be happy that other people are dead. No matter how much they might deserve it. And it isn't rational to be happy that a man like Simon is alive." Her arms tightened, crushing her daughter protectively against her chest. "In times like this... the most you can be is relieved."

Rae caught her breath and nodded. Relieved all over again just to have gotten it all off her chest. But when they pulled way, her voice was soft as a whisper. "But you're not."

It was a throwaway line. One designed only to provoke a response.

Beth sighed and returned to the dishes, wiping them dry with a robotic efficiency. "No, Rae. I can never be relieved that Simon's alive. Not after what he's done. Not after..."

Carter.

The unspoken name rang out between them, and for a second it felt like neither one could catch their breath. Beth's entire body flinched, as if a giant weight had been dropped upon her, and without seeming to think about it she cradled the hand with her diamond ring.

"Mom, I—"

But then Beth was off. Breezing from the kitchen without another word. Leaving a stack of dripping dishes behind her.

Under normal circumstances, Rae would have let her go. Under normal circumstances, she would have bent over backwards to give her mother all the space she needed to work through this unspeakable grief. Under normal circumstances, she would have turned back to the sink and finished doing the dishes herself.

Except that Beth hadn't left the kitchen empty-handed. She'd taken a knife.

"Mom?!" Rae tore after her, dropping the plate she'd been holding onto the tile floor. She could still hear it shattering as she raced through the living room to the back hallway that led to the basement.

But Beth wasn't there.

Confused and panting Rae froze in place, whirling around as if at any moment she might pop back into sight. There was a faint buzzing in her skin as her body switched automatically to a handy tracking tatù—curtesy of Ellie's boyfriend, Jake. She had never used the ink before, but the premise seemed simple.

Sure enough, the second she focused on her mother her exact location floated through Rae's head. But what the... Her mother had taken a knife and run to the bathroom?!

It was even worse than Rae had thought!

"MOM!" she screamed, switching ink again to the raw power of Jennifer's leopard.

Why, of all the moments in the world, did she have to pick *that exact one* for a spontaneous confession?! She felt *relieved*?! When her mother had just lost the only man she'd ever really loved?! Of course she was high-tailing it to the bathroom with a blade! Rae could only hope she'd get there in time. Panic seized her lungs and she tried to breathe around it.

"MOM!" She flew up the stairs, five at a time. "Don't you *dare* do anything—"

But a second before she could kick down the door, it opened by itself.

Beth stood just inside the frame, staring at her curiously. The sharpened blade in one hand, a can of shaving cream in the other. "Rae?" She lifted her eyebrows with motherly concern. "Are you okay, honey?"

The world slowed back down into focus as Rae tried slowly to catch her breath. Over the last few years, she had learned not to take chances with sudden departures and sharp objects. But looking at her mother now, her blind panic seemed a bit premature. "Yeah, of course." She casually leaned against the doorframe and blew a lock of hair up out of her face. "Uh...what're you doing?"

The hint of a smile tugged at Beth's lips, but she kept a straight face.

"We can't have Anthony Fodder meeting with a man who, I can only presume, looks like the last Alcatraz survivor." She held up the shaving cream. "Do you think Devon will mind?"

It took a second for Rae to switch tracks. Her eyes flickered cartoonishly between the can and the blade before coming to rest on her mother. "Not, not at all but...you're going to *shave* him?"

And ironic smile flitted across Beth's face as she examined the sharpened knife with a hint of satisfaction. "Someone's got to, and I can't trust him with a razor."

"Yeah, but...do you need to use a carving knife?"

"Relax, honey." Beth patted Rae's shoulder as she headed down the stairs. "Mommy and Daddy are just going to have a little chat..."

"—and then she went down into the basement. And I haven't heard from her since." Rae nervously wrung her hands, terrified she had done the wrong thing.

The war games in the front yard had come to an abrupt halt when she had summoned her friends inside with a single, telepathic shriek. Their reactions to such things had been programmed the same as hers and in no time at all they were back in their ring of chairs.

"I'm sure they're just talking," Molly said soothingly. "You heard your mom when we stopped her the first time. It'll all work out." Molly flicked her hair over her shoulder. "We don't kill people in cold blood."

There was a derisive snort behind her as Angel folded her arms across her chest. "That is, without a doubt, the *stupidest* thing you have ever said." The sardonic blonde had woken up about ten minutes before with a splitting headache, only to remember what had made her go out and drink in the first place. She wasn't exactly taking it well.

Molly flashed her a glare before turning suddenly smug. "It wasn't me who said it—it was your brother."

Angel glanced at Gabriel, looking deeply disturbed, then shrugged dismissively. "He was drunk."

"He was *right*," Julian corrected firmly. His beloved might blur the lines on occasion, but on this point they all had to be absolutely clear. "We don't kill for revenge. We all know that." He lifted his eyes to Rae. "And Beth does, too. Don't worry. She knows what she's doing."

Rae nodded quickly, but couldn't seem to slow down her racing heart. No matter what she did, she couldn't get the image out of her head: her mother standing behind the interrogation chair in the basement, holding a carving knife to her father's throat.

Whether there was shaving cream present didn't make much of a difference.

"I know, it's just..." She bit her lip. "Will you check for me, Jules?"

"*Rae!*" Angel snapped.

Even Devon gave her a surprised look, but she was undeterred. The others might not have seen it, but Julian had already used his power once before. To make sure Molly would be safe, when Simon first walked into the bathroom. Surely he could use it again—just for this.

The psychic looked uncertain.

"I don't..." He paused and started again. "Rae, I'm sure it's going to be fine."

"Yeah, it is, babe." Devon caught her arm, putting a stop to her frantic pacing. "If you like, I can even go to the door to check."

"No," Rae stopped him quickly. "This is the first time the two of them are talking in over a decade. I mean, think about it. They're still technically married, for Pete's sake! They deserve a little privacy. I just..." She caught her breath, "Jules, I just don't want to lift the turkey tray cover tomorrow at dinner and find my dad's head on a silver platter." Before anyone could shoot the idea down, she echoed her words from before. "Stranger things have happened."

Julian sighed and pulled his hair back away from his face. A little ash fell to the floor after his run-in with the flamethrower. "Just this once," he warned. "That's it, Kerrigan."

"Just this once," she echoed, lifting to her toes in anticipation.

He took a deep breath, steeled himself against the tiles, just as they had done so many times before his eyes glassed over to an iridescent white.

It was strange. Rae had seen him do this so many times over the years, it had almost become second nature. But it wasn't until seeing it now that she realized how long it had been.

Just this once, she told herself. *And it hasn't been that long. Only seven days.*

But in so many ways, it felt a lot longer.

The ghostly eyes and clairvoyant sight that allowed Julian to peer into the future may have stroked out your average spectator, but to people like Rae and her friends, people with tatùs, it was as natural as breathing.

What *wasn't* natural was suppression of that ink.

Without boasting, Rae could honestly say that Julian was the most gifted psychic to have ever walked the planet. Time had a looser grip on him that it did on the others. He could see between the worlds by merely opening his eyes. Unlock a thousand uncharted futures and dimensions by simply willing it so. She couldn't begin to imagine what it was like for him to have stayed grounded in the present for so long.

Sure enough, the second he 'tranced out,' as the others like to call it, his entire body relaxed with the deepest feeling of relief. It was like watching someone finally coming up for air after having been trapped underwater for so long.

But before she could take any comfort in that fact, his entire expression changed. Usually, he was just blank. It didn't matter whether he was seeing the outcome of a sports match, or the end of the world. There wouldn't be a shred of emotion on his face to clue you in.

This was a bit different. He was already beginning to frown by the time his eyes cleared.

"Jules?" As usual Devon stepped forward first, standing side by side with Angel as they looked him over with concern. "What is it? What did you see?"

Instead of answering, Julian turned his head towards the front door. The others followed suit. No sooner had they done so than the doorbell rang.

"Who is it?" Molly asked, shrinking back. Luke took her by the hand, and without seeming to think about it the two of them started backing up the stairs. "Knights? Council?"

Julian just stared in shock for another moment before slowly shaking his head. A look of utter disbelief flitted across his face, then his lips turned up with a wry smile.

"Just answer the door, Rae," he muttered, bracing himself for yet another unimaginable twist of fate. "I wouldn't want to spoil the surprise."

With a feeling of great trepidation, Rae walked slowly to the door. If it was anything dangerous, Julian wouldn't have let her do it. But 'not dangerous' didn't necessarily mean 'not bad.'

Just do it, Rae. You asked for it.

She yanked it open before she could stop herself, squaring her shoulders with the grit of someone who'd had to do this sort of thing too many times before.

But nothing in the world could have prepared Rae for what happened next.

She stared, her mouth hanging open.

People moved behind her to see who was there.

"Kraigan?!" Rae blinked and made an effort to try to close her mouth.

Her half-brother looked up at her with a lopsided grin, his arms held securely behind his back by a small squadron of police.

"I got your message, and here I am!" he said proudly, seemingly unaware that he was dripping a steady pool of blood onto the front porch. "And a day early, I might add."

Rae couldn't seem to get her mouth to close. Couldn't do anything other than gape in shock at what had to be the cruelest timing the cosmos had yet to provide.

"My... my message?" she repeated in shock, trying to summon back her senses.

After getting a permissive look from the nearest officer holding him, he reached into his back pocket and pulled out a rumpled card. Even from where she stood, Rae could see the blood-stained turkey.

"Happy Thanksgiving, sis. It's going to be one for the books."

Chapter 13

Rae locked her eyes onto the decorative little turkey like it had come from hell itself. "I didn't give you that," she said accusingly. As if by simply denying the problem existed it might have the decency to go away. "Where the heck did you get that, Kraigan? I never sent you an invitation. I don't even know where you live at the moment!"

His smile turned grim. "An oversight—I presume. Anyway, I found it when I raided Gabriel's apartment the other night. Decided to stop on by and say hello."

"You raided my apartment?" Gabriel asked sharply.

At this, Kraigan looked remarkably sincere. "Yeah, dude. I was hoping you might want to hang out? You know, like back in Scotland?"

Gabriel was unmoved. "How do you know where I live?"

Kraigan shrugged, not looking the least bit sheepish. "I have my ways."

Rae threw up her hands. "Not the point, Kraigan. Why did you—"

"I'm sorry to interrupt this little family dispute," an officer interrupted rudely, sounding not sorry at all, "but are you Rachel Kerrigan?"

The entire gang blinked in unison, staring at the officer.

Well, I've never heard that one before...

"Uh, it's Rae, actually." She nervously tucked her wavy hair behind her ears. For a blissful moment, she had somehow forgotten about the police standing at her door. "What seems to be—"

"I thought Rae was short for Rachel," the officer insisted, as if it could have possibly mattered less.

For a second, she almost went along with it. If for no other reason than to expedite things.

"Sorry, no. But is there something I could...I could help you with, Officer?" She felt ridiculous. Like she was reading lines out of a play.

The entire squadron seemed to swell with importance as they shoved Kraigan a step or two forward.

The man, who Rae was certain still thought her name was Rachel, took the lead. "We responded to a local disturbance a few days ago; turned out to be a bit bigger than we thought. Protocol says that after releasing unclaimed persons from a seventy-two-hour hold, we're required to deliver them to next of kin." He cocked his head towards Kraigan, who was watching Rae with a sly smile. "He says he's related to you?"

That son of a bitch. Of course he did. The one time he'll claim me as his family, without denying it outright, has to be the day that he's released from a psychiatric hold.

Rae was too busy fuming to answer, so reinforcements—aka her friends—swooped in to the rescue.

"His family's dead," Angel replied unfeelingly. "He's a bloody orphan. Take him away. I'm sure you have a facility where you can permanently lock up people like him."

For possibly the first time ever, Devon looked like he wanted to give Angel a high-five.

But despite the general urge to agree with her sentiment, the others had the self-control to at least keep it to themselves. Things had changed after the 'battle to save the world.' Alliances had been replaced with friendships. Friendships had been replaced with family. There were some things that bonded you, with ties so strong they could never be broken.

No matter how much you might want to.

"What happened?" Rae didn't direct her question at the police, but at Kraigan himself. While the stakes might have been as high as they came, he responded like his signature, flippant self.

"You know," he shrugged, "just the usual. I'm a danger to myself and others. A general menace to society. I need to be "stopped" and somehow "controlled". You know how it goes."

He actually used sarcastic little air-quotes when he said "stopped" and "controlled". Rae decided killing him right then might be his best option. Except for that little thing about immortality. If he still had Cromfield's ink, it would be too effective. She shrugged. It might be worth a try.

Fortunately, the policeman stepped in between.

"We found him jumping in front of a train at Waterloo Station."

It took a lot to surprise Rae at this point, but that did the trick.

"Kraigan?"

He answered her fearful question with a knowing smirk, kicking his feet to deliberately scuff up their porch. A second later, a burst of understanding narrowed Rae's eyes.

Testing the limits of his newfound immortality, is he?

"We asked him if he was trying to commit suicide, but he flat-out denied it," the officer continued. When this made no impact he leaned forward, enunciating every word to really drive the point home. "Apparently, he didn't think it would hurt him."

It would have hurt, alright. Just not killed him.

Unfortunately, the same couldn't be said for the other people on the train.

"And what about the passengers?" Rae asked sharply, eyes locked on her brother. "Kraigan? What about the other people on the train?"

It was hard to say if he heard her or not. He was too busy staring at the twisted hunk of metal that used to be the lawnmower, sitting in the middle of the yard.

"You guys have been busy," he murmured.

The officer threw up his hands in exasperation. Between Rae's rather cryptic responses and Kraigan's downright lunacy, he obviously thought that madness must run in the family. "Clearly, the boy is delusional."

Rae ground her teeth together. "Clearly."

"However," he continued, "since he technically passed the psychological evaluation, we have no legitimate grounds to hold him. We simply came to release him into your care."

"Good." She nodded firmly. A second passed. "Wait—what?"

It was then that she noticed the suitcase.

"According to Statute 248 of the NHS Trust—"

"Yeah, yeah," Rae waved her hands in front of her like a shield, "that's all well and good, except... he can't stay here. Not right now."

Kraigan's eyes lit with automatic curiosity, but the policeman saw nothing but the refusal.

"Listen, *Ms.* Kerrigan," he was practically sneering, ready to wash his hands of the whole dysfunctional lot, "what's going to happen next is I'm going to un-cuff him, get in my car, drive away, and never think about your little family ever again. Do you understand?"

Great! Now even commoners were coming to hate the family name.

Rae hesitated, weighed her options, then went out on a limb.

"Do you have to take off the cuffs?"

The officer simply glared as he removed the restraints. "Have a nice day. And try to stay out of trouble."

The squad car shot down the drive in a cloud of dust, leaving brother and sister facing off in the gravel behind them. Trapped in the world's most unwanted reunion.

"So," he began with a wide smile while he rubbed his bruised wrists, "why exactly is *now* such a bad time?"

He can't go inside. He can't go inside. He can't go inside.

Rae chanted it over and over in her head. Like a reaffirming anthem. Maybe if she simply said it enough it would have to come true. But each time came out weaker than the last. In the end, it morphed into a lesser compromise altogether.

He can't go in the basement. He can't go in the basement. He can't go in the basement.

"Well, I didn't exactly expect you guys to roll out the welcome mat, but shit!" Kraigan strode forward, ignoring the way everyone automatically cringed out of reach. "Look at your faces! What happened? We facing a looming apocalypse again?"

No one could bring themselves to answer. They had no way of knowing it, but they were all currently chanting the same thing. Rae knew it.

Not in the basement! Not in the basement! Not in the basement!

"I would have at least expected more from you." He clapped Julian on the shoulder before he could move out of range. "What? You didn't see me coming?"

Julian peeled himself slowly out from under his hand. "I literally just did... not in time to leave the country."

Kraigan threw back his head, laughing as if they were the oldest of friends. "There's the psychic I know and love! Still funny as ever!" He gazed around the little circle with what looked like genuine excitement. "The lame boyfriend. My almost-bromace. The white-haired bitch, and the red-haired witch. And...you!" He came to stop on Luke. "Truth be told, I always kind of liked you. Although I can never remember your name."

The gang shared a long look, none of them knowing what to do.

"Come on—enough already!" Kraigan grinned, flashing every one of his teeth. "Tell me everything that's been happening! I've missed this!"

Guys...I have to tell him.

Rae sent out the message telepathically to everyone at the same time, hoping to get back a feeling of general consensus. She received a variety of responses instead.

Devon frowned. Angel cursed and spat on the ground. Gabriel shook his head. Julian lifted a shoulder in a tentative shrug. Luke looked at Molly.

And Molly shot her with lightning.

Rae slowly lifted herself off the ground, trying for round two.

There's no way around it. He's going to find out one way or another.

Devon frowned even deeper. Angel took a mad swipe at Rae. Gabriel and Julian caught her by the wrist. Luke looked at Molly.

And Molly shot her with lightning.

Come on! Enough already!

"Dude, Red—chill out."

Molly turned around in slow motion to see Kraigan shaking his head chidingly. "I'm sorry, sewer rat—did you say something?"

He lifted his head sagely. "Violence is never the answer."

There was a *zing*, followed by a sharp *hiss*.

"Molly!" Angel congratulated. "That was your best bolt ever!"

It was a rare moment of bonding for the two, but it was cut short as quickly as it started.

"Kraigan, you can't go inside because Beth's in there," Devon interrupted suddenly.

It was like a beam of light came down from the sky, illuminating another option that none of them had been able to see.

Rae looked up hopefully, and for a second Kraigan actually paused.

"Beth?" For the first time, he sounded a bit uncertain. "You think I shouldn't go inside because... she doesn't want to see me?"

"No one ever wants to see you, Kraigan," Angel said rudely. "I, for one, think that you had the right idea going with the train."

Julian closed his eyes painfully, and Devon pushed her forward into the dirt.

Kraigan, however, seemed to take her words to heart. He ignored the little scuffle between them completely, and focused on Rae instead.

"Is she really that upset that I didn't go to the funeral?"

It was in that second that Rae made up her mind. That second of rare vulnerability that tilted the scales permanently in Kraigan's favor. Because even so vulnerable, even laying all his cards out on the line—he still managed to lie.

He *did* go to the funeral. Rae had seen him there.

He wasn't standing with the rest of them, of course. In fact, Rae wouldn't have been surprised if she was the only one to have seen him. He was standing on the far other side of the field, gazing out over the proceedings with a blank expression on his face.

There was a reason that Molly and Angel were so quick to condemn. Likewise, there was a reason that Gabriel and Devon were withholding open violence.

The girls hadn't been with Cromfield that night. The boys had.

As much as Rae hated him, as much as she might despise every single infuriating thing about him... Kraigan had been brave that night. He saved their lives. As surely as Carter did himself.

She hadn't told anyone about the funeral. If Kraigan didn't want people to know he had gone, that was his business. Truth be told, she'd even forgotten to tell Devon.

But she knew. And he knew. And that was enough.

"Is that a legitimate invitation?" she asked.

He looked down at the blood-soaked turkey in his hand, then waved it in the air.

"Then I guess you're coming inside."

"WHAT?!" Molly and Angel screamed it at the same time. The boys were staring with similar looks of dismay. Only Devon kept his eyes steadily on Rae instead.

She pulled herself up to her full height, staring at each one of them in turn.

"My *brother*," she emphasized it as much as she could stand, "can stay."

And so it was decided.

The others disbursed quietly, glaring with various levels of malice as they headed back into the house. But before Kraigan could follow, Rae grabbed him by the arm and pulled him close.

"There are three things. Do you hear me?" She lowered her voice so that no one else could hear. "Three rules you're going to abide by if you're living in this house."

His lips turned up in a sarcastic smile as he peered down at the top of her head. It was always harder to do the 'big sister' thing when your brother was over six feet.

Rae gritted her teeth together, but held firm. "First: you go easy on them."

"Go easy?" He actually looked surprised. "What do you mean?"

Rae looked him straight in the eye. "I'm not joking here, Kraigan. No more games. No messing around. These people have gone through *hell*. Do you get that? Total. Absolute. Hell. They did not emerge the same on the other side." She would have given anything for it not to be true, but at this point there was no denying it. "They're trying to get past it. They're trying to heal. What they *do not* need is the added headache of you being in this house."

"So what am I supposed to—"

"Don't be a headache."

He jutted his chin up stiffly, but nodded his head. "I'll try my best."

She gave him a long look.

"Fine. I'll do slightly better than that."

"Rule number two: no more trying to kill yourself for fun."

This one seemed too much to bear.

"Oh, come on, Rae!" He threw up his hands. "You can't legitimately ask me that. Didn't you do it when you first got the power?"

Breathe in through your nose, out through your mouth. Then maybe, just maybe, you won't strangle him.

She opened her eyes with a glare.

Or maybe you will. Either way, at least you tried.

"These people have seen enough death and bloodshed in the last two days to last them several lifetimes. I'm not going to have them wake up andwalk downstairs to get coffee, only to see you trying to dismember yourself on the lawn. I'm serious, alright? Do it on your own time."

He scuffed his shoes once more against the pavement. "Fine, fine. Whatever."

She put her hands on her hips, feeling vaguely satisfied with his compliance before spotting the fallen handcuffs on the ground.

"And for the record, Kraigan, that whole 'big sister bails you out with the cops' bit? That's the last family bonding you and I are going to have, got it?"

His lips curled back in a sneer. "As if I would want anything else." They shared another glare before he glanced at the house impatiently. "So, what's next?"

"What?"

"The third rule. You said you had three."

"Oh..." Rae hesitated, following his gaze as a nervous swarm of butterflies began pounding away in her stomach. "The third rule is just... try to have an open mind."

He shot her a questioning glance. "Really? That's your big finale? An open mind?"

She nodded.

"What the hell is that even supposed to mean?" he pressed.

"Nothing, just...you'll see." She back-pedaled quickly. "I mean, keep it in mind. You never know where the day is going to take you."

Even though he was the one newly released from a psychiatric hold, he looked at her like *she* might be crazy. Fortunately, with Kraigan crazy was never a deal-breaker.

"Whatever you say, sis." With that, he clapped her on the shoulder and headed inside, having no idea what in the world might await him.

Rae picked up his forgotten bag and dragged it behind them, eyes fixed on the back of his head.

You never know where the day is going to take you...

It was the second time Rae had to sit through a 'post-incarceration' meal with her little brother. Watching him scarf down ungodly amounts of pasta, speckling the floor with dots of marinara. She could only hope it would be the last.

Angel still resolutely wasn't talking to her for letting Kraigan come inside, but Molly had come around. Best friends could only stay mad at each other for so long. She, too, was perched at the end of the dining room table, eyeing the spectacle with a growing level of disgust.

"*Aaaand* that does it," she declared, watching him tilt back his head to inhale a noodle. "I think my morning sickness just came back."

"Morning sickness?" He surfaced just long enough to tune into the conversation. "You're pregnant? For real?"

She hesitated, unable to believe she'd just given it away.

"Is that dude the father? The one with the mohawk?" He shot her a quizzical look. "What's his name again?"

"His name is Luke, Kraigan." Rae rubbed her eyes. "You've only met him like a hundred times. You've freaking lived with him—"

"You're going to be an awesome mother."

The kitchen fell abruptly silent. Only occasional slurping sounds broke through as Kraigan returned to his meal.

Molly shot Rae a bewildered look before they turned back. "You...you really think so?"

"Absolutely!" he declared through a mouth full of noodles. "A lot better than this one's going to be."

He cocked his head towards Rae, but at the last second he added a wink. Her automatic snarl twisted up into a begrudging grin. Rule number one. He was trying.

Now if he could just manage to follow the rest of them...

"Well, I'm stuffed." He kicked back his chair, tossing his plate into the sink with a careless clatter. "Where should I drop my bag? Which room is mine?"

Rae quickly got up to follow him as he wandered out into the hall, unwilling to let him out of her sight. "Well, the thing is, Kraigan, before we get you all settled in there's actually something we wanted to..."

Both brother and sister froze at the same time.

A man had emerged from the basement. A man who looked nothing like the man who had gone in. This man was clean and refined. Handsome, even. With a charming smile and a pair of sparkling eyes that fixed upon his children the second they walked into the room.

Beth had come up behind him, looking alert but confident at the same time. In a way, she almost looked relaxed. As if a fifteen-year-old weight had been lifted from her chest.

She, too, stopped when she saw the children.

For a moment, the four of them just stood there. Trapped in another strange family reunion.

Maybe he won't recognize him. Rae cast a sideways glance at Kraigan. *He was just four or five years old when Simon 'died.' Maybe he's not going to—*

But it was as if Kraigan had been struck with a bolt of lightning. The second he saw Simon his feet froze, but every nerve in his body lit up like a live wire.

He took a tentative step forward, as if trying to get a better view, before his face broke into the brightest smile Rae had ever seen.

"Holy shit! ...*Dad*?"

Chapter 14

"YOU'RE ALIVE!"

There was a blur of moment as Kraigan leapt into Simon with the biggest embrace Rae had ever seen. The two men went barreling backwards, stumbling with the force of it before Simon managed to hold Kraigan—in a hug and still on his feet.

Rae looked on in shock. Beth, with eyes probably as big as Rae's, watched them embrace.

Simon slowly lowered his hands, placing them tentatively on his son's back. "...Kraigan?"

The two of them pulled back, looking each other up and down.

At first, it was easy to understand the question in Simon's voice. While there weren't many people in the world who could call him 'Dad', Kraigan was a different person than the boy he'd left.

To start, they were the same height now. Both towering at something over six feet. Tall, yes, but in this household they were in good company. They both had the same color hair. An odd shade of brown—lighter at certain times of day, darker in others. Curly and changeable, depending on where they were. Now that they were standing face to face, it was also easy to see that they had the same mouth. And the same chin. The same a lot of things. Particularly the same tatù.

Come to think of it... Rae didn't look much like her father at all. It was just Kraigan.

It's for the best, she thought, edging towards her mother. *That's not exactly the kind of face you want to be walking around with in this part of the world. I may have his hair... and his ink, too.*

Kraigan didn't seem to mind that he looked just like his father. In fact, he looked overjoyed just at the prospect. Rae had never seen him so beside himself, soaking in every detail with rapturous attention.

"You're so..." Simon shook his head incredulously. "You're all grown up."

Coincidentally, he was also the only person in the house who didn't hesitate in the slightest before touching Simon's skin. For a second, Rae fought the urge to pull them apart. The last thing they needed to add to the 'Kerrigan problem' was a supernatural dose of immortality.

Kraigan bounced from foot to foot, the psychiatric identification tags still rattling on his wrists. "Just a year younger than Rae!" He flashed her a quick smile, seemingly unaware of the adulterous implication he'd just made right in front of Beth. "But I don't understand—how is this possible? You died in that fire... I saw it myself."

It was true. Although only two people present had actually lived through the horrors of that fateful day, all of them had seen it courtesy of one of Rae's tatùs.

"You *saw* it?" Simon asked with a hint of confusion. "How is *that* possible?"

"Rae showed me," Kraigan answered carelessly, far less concerned with the issues of the past than he was with the delights of the present. "Used her tatù." He glanced down at his own before his eyes shot over to his father's, covered by his shirt.

Simon leaned back in surprise, glancing appraisingly at Rae. "Did she now...?"

Rae could almost see him tabulating. Counting up the things he'd seen so far.

First there was the super speed, then there was the conjuring. And now he'd learned that she could see the past.

She could see the wheels turning in his head. *Three* abilities? That couldn't be right, could it?

His eyes flickered curiously to Beth and then quickly back to his daughter, but Kraigan bounced in between them. Like an over-excited child who couldn't get enough attention.

"So how did you do it, Dad?" Kraigan had no problem using the word. Rae found that it continued to stick in her throat. "How did you make it out of the fire?"

Simon stared between his children for another moment before sliding his hands inside his pockets. "Not of my own volition, I'm afraid. I was taken prisoner by a man named Jonathon Cromfield. Yet another person long presumed dead, except—"

"—Except he was a hybrid gifted with both sight and immortality," Rae interrupted, moving things along quicker. "We know."

"Wait—*Cromfield* had you all along?!" Kraigan exclaimed, his brows pressing together. "You were in the factory?" He glanced behind to Rae for confirmation. "Same factory, right? That's how you found him?"

She nodded silently as Simon frowned.

"Hold on." He swallowed. "How do you all know Jonathon Cromfield?"

For a moment the conversation stopped as all three of them— Beth included—turned to gaze at Simon with the slightest bit of pity.

In their quest to satiate their own curiosity, in their haste to answer of all their burning questions—they'd forgotten that Simon must have some burning questions of his own. In fact, given that they could find out almost anything they wanted know between the newspapers and the case files, it was likely that he had a hell of a lot more questions than they did.

He simply didn't know anything. Not anymore. His entire life was in the past. It had effectively ended the day Cromfield dragged him out of that fire. Everything since then had been just passing time. A mindless purgatory in which the rest of the world went on without him.

"We..." Rae paused, wondering where to begin. "I guess you could say we crossed paths."

"I killed him," Kraigan announced proudly, ever his father's hero.

Unable to control herself, Rae rolled her eyes and folded her arms across her chest. "Oh, *you* did, did you? It wasn't the fact that Devon buried a dagger in his chest?"

Kraigan's nostrils flared. "Only after *I* stripped the man of every tatù in his arsenal. You know that dagger wouldn't have worked if it wasn't for me!"

Rae snorted. "Yeah? It also wouldn't have worked if Gabriel hadn't held him steady so long," Rae shot back, unwilling to surrender the credit for such an incredible victory to only one person. Not when so many had given so much. "And it also wouldn't have worked if I hadn't spent the last ten minutes knocking him senseless with everything I had!"

"Oh, that's just like you, isn't it?" Kraigan spat, towering over her as the two of them squared off. "Little Miss Privy Council President always has to save the day!"

Rae stretched up on her toes in frustration. "I'm not saying that I alone saved the day! I'm just saying that it took a hell of a lot of people to bring him down, and you can't—"

"Children!"

Both Beth and Simon shouted at the same time. Then they turned to share the strangest look that Rae had ever seen.

Looks like we're having a family Thanksgiving after all...

Beth took a wide step away from Simon as he cleared his throat quickly, hastening to get the shaky conversation back on track. "Is that why you were voted President of the Privy Council?" he asked Rae with an unmistakable note of pride. "After killing Cromfield in the factory?"

It sounded like he didn't know what was more impossible: The fact that Jonathon Cromfield, his immortal counterpart, was truly dead, or the fact that his long-lost daughter was actually the leader of the supernatural government.

Rae was about to answer, when Kraigan stepped forward again, unwilling to share even an ounce of the spotlight. "Yeah, Rae went the conventional route," he replied, sounding distinctly unimpressed. "Until very recently, I was actually a fugitive—like you."

Rae grimaced on his behalf, while Beth stepped forward with a sudden frown.

"Kraigan. What exactly are you doing here?"

"Oh," his hand lifted in a wave welcome, "I just got out of prison. See," he flashed his father a wink, "I told you we have a lot in common."

Rae fought back a wave of nausea.

Beth pressed on, not understanding why a secluded mansion in Kent would have automatically been his first stop. "Did you come here for Thanksgiving?"

"Thanksgiving," Simon interjected with surprise. "It's November?" Then he glanced around with a touch of confusion. "Why in the world are we celebrating Thanksgiving? Is that an English thing now as well? Have we been re-colonized?"

Beth shot him a truly indecipherable look. "Your daughter grew up in New York, with her uncle. She's American. Celebrates American holidays."

Simon absorbed this for a moment, before his face tightened in shock. "Why did Argyle raise her in America? Where the hell were you?"

"Supposedly dead, according to Rae." Beth's voice began to rise.

"You're here now. Back then, you were happy to lock me away—"

Rae closed her eyes as the two of them began shouting out of control.

It was going to be a family Thanksgiving alright.

After the altercation in the living room, everyone retreated to their separate corners for a much- needed break. Simon was returned to the basement. Beth went out for a drive to clear her head. Rae went upstairs to unload her feelings upon her unsuspecting fiancé.

And Kraigan... Rae had no idea where he'd gone, nor did anyone else.

"He was just so *happy* to see him," she repeated for the seventh time, pacing like a madman in front of the bed. "Like it was his own Thanksgiving miracle. He smiled! It freakin' reached his eyes. He was like, "Wahoo! Our father's really alive.""

Devon was laid out on top of the bed, propped up against the headboard. He tracked her progress carefully, glancing down on occasion to see if she was actually wearing a trail into the floor. "Well, you know Kraigan's always idolized your dad. That's no big surprise. And as for the other thing..." His voice and eyes gentled at the same time. "Honey, you might not have been thrilled that your dad was alive, but you can't tell me that at least some small part of you wasn't—"

"Relieved?" Rae interrupted, casting him a quick look. "Yeah, don't remind me. I said the exact same thing to my mom this afternoon."

Devon leaned back in surprise. "You told Beth that you were relieved Simon wasn't dead?"

Rae sank down where she stood, her face in her hands. "Yeah. I did. Genius move, right?"

In a second he was sitting on the floor beside her, fingers lacing gently through her own.

"It's...surprising, to be sure." She looked up and he gave her a crooked smile. "Hey, no one ever said you Kerrigans were predictable. But at least it was honest."

She looked down with a sigh but he squeezed her hand, bringing her back to attention.

"I'm serious, Rae. It was honest. It's good you said it. Just like when you stopped her from going down to the basement. It might not have been what she wanted to hear... but it was the right thing to do. No matter which way you look at it." He stroked back her long hair, cupping her face in his hands. "You've got a beautiful heart, Rae. It's one of the first things I fell in love with. Of course you're relieved that your dad is alive. Of course you're doing everything in your power to protect him now that he's here." His face lit up with a sudden smile. "Actually, I guess it's not that surprising after all. That's just you."

Rae placed her hand over his before turning her head to kiss his palm. "I almost told her today," she whispered. "I couldn't help myself. Every time I see her, it gets harder and harder to keep it a secret."

At this, Devon dropped his eyes to his lap. His shoulders stiffened with automatic tension before falling with a tired sigh. "I know. It's hard for me, too."

The decision not to tell Beth about their engagement had been universal. Echoed by every single one of their friends. It had started with the crack of a bullet, and had solidified by the time Carter's body was carried out of the room.

They could not advertise this kind of happiness. Not right now. Not like this. And especially not now that the sky had started falling once again.

"We'll do it soon." He kissed her finger where the ring was supposed to be. "I promise. And until then..." He pulled out his wallet and tipped it over into his palm. A sparkling diamond fell into his open hand, sending up rays of light all over the room. "I'll keep this with me day and night."

They leaned towards each other. Closed their eyes. Parted their lips.

Then suddenly all hell broke loose.

CRASH!

A shadowy figure fell from the top of the dresser, landing with a muffled profanity in the middle of the floor. As Rae and Devon leapt to their feet with a cry, the figure began to change color. The chestnut grains of browns and odd antique-looking hues lightening to a flat grey trench coat and a pair of slacks. Complete with prison ID tags.

"*Kraigan!*" Rae screamed, ready to kill him.

He scrambled to his feet just in time to dodge the bolt of lightning from his sister's hand. A second bolt was soon to follow, providing cover fire as Devon stuffed the precious ring back into his pocket.

"It's not what you think!" he cried, shielding his face with his hands. "I wasn't going to hurt anyone. I was only spying! Using the other half of my own tatù. Nothing stolen! Nothing sinister!"

The bolt that followed left a small crater in the wood. But before she could surrender to her darker temptations and finally barbeque her little brother like she'd always wanted, he dropped his hands completely and said the one thing that could get her to stop.

"You're getting married?"

For once, there wasn't an ounce of malice on his face. No evil flicker, no hint at a deep, dark plan. Not a trace of that cocky smile they all knew and hated so well.

All the darkness had cleared away to leave him looking strangely childlike, staring at his big sister in a state of wide-eyed shock.

"Devon asked you to marry him?"

For a second, the lightning paused. The fire-poker Devon had grabbed lowered slowly in his hand as the three of them froze in momentary silence.

"I don't..." Rae began, but there was no point in denying it. He had already heard them talking. He had already seen the ring. Instead, she shared a quick look with Devon before instinctively clutching her hand. "He proposed a few days before the battle," she murmured, silently wondering in what kind of world did she tell Kraigan this information before telling her own mother.

Kraigan just stood there, looking downright astonished. "And...you said yes?"

Both Rae and Devon shot him a sour look, and he was quick to back-pedal.

"No. I didn't meant it like that. Of course you said yes, it's just..." His eyes met his sister's, and for one of the first times in their lives he offered her a genuine smile. "Congratulations, Rae."

Congratulations?! Okay, what kind of alternate dimension have I stumbled upon...

"Uh... Thank you?"

This time, it was her turn to look shocked. Devon instinctively raised the fire-poker back up again, but brother and sister were having their own little moment. Oblivious to the rest of the world.

They simply stood there for a moment, cautiously feeling out these first tentative steps of 'family' before Rae crossed the room and did the most surprising thing of all.

She gave him a hug.

"Rae—*Don't.*" Kraigan made a strange, strangled sound and stiffened up as straight as a board, closing his eyes and wincing as if she might just go away. When that didn't work, he actually tried pushing her off of him, but without his usual ink she was far too strong. "What the hell are—"

"Just stand there," she soothed. "Just let it happen."

Blame it on the fact that she'd just bailed out her little brother with the cops. Blame it on the fact that she'd just seen him transform into what she could only describe as a 'giddy five-year-old boy' the second he saw his long-lost father. Blame it on the damn congratulations on their engagement.

Whatever the reason... this hug was a long time coming.

"I think I'm having a panic attack," he muttered. "An actual panic attack."

She grinned, squeezing him even tighter. "Remember, if you take my strength tatù you won't be immortal."

He looked like he was seriously considering it anyway. "This is the worst thing that's ever happened to me. Worse than prison."

She patted him consolingly on the back of the head. "You're going to learn to love it."

Then a sudden flash illuminated the room, and both siblings sprang back to their opposite corners. Devon was already slipping his phone back into his pocket—but judging by the quiet *dings* echoing from all corners of the house, he'd already texted the photographic evidence to everyone he knew. He returned their murderous expressions with a satisfied smile. "Come on! *No one* would have believed me otherwise."

"On second thought," Kraigan aggressively shifted forward, "you could do a lot better."

Rae's eyes narrowed as she mimicked his move. "I'm beginning to think you're right."

Devon gulped and took a cautious step back, glancing between the two as if assessing a threat he never would have imagined was possible. "*Anyway*," he said causally, "we should probably get back downstairs..."

Rae rolled her eyes, but allowed him his transparent escape. She snatched her sweater up off the floor, but as she made to follow Kraigan caught her elbow and held her back.

"You're really," he paused, sounding almost shy, "you're really not happy he's back?"

Her whole body stiffened, then wilted with a weary sigh. Unable to say the words for a second time, she simply shook her head. He absorbed this for a moment.

"But you also stopped your mom from killing him?"

Again, words failed her. She merely nodded.

A cloud of confusion flickered across Kraigan's face, darkening to a sort of burning frustration as he tried to understand. "How could you not be happy? He's our dad."

At this, Devon stepped graciously outside to give them a moment as Rae turned around with another stifled sigh. "He killed a lot of people, Kraigan. *Killed* them."

Kraigan's face went blank, making it impossible to determine his verdict. "But he's our *dad*."

Rae bit her lip as she stared up into those dark eyes. For the first time, they seemed as searching as her own. Piercing deep down into her own, trying to answer an impossible question. "And that's why I saved his life."

It was a very 'Kerrigan' ending to the conversation, but an ending nonetheless. One that both she and Kraigan were satisfied with—at least for the time being. They headed down the stairs together, not seeming to realize the usual barrier of space between them had been subconsciously bridged.

It wasn't until they reached the kitchen that Rae pulled him to a stop. "Kraigan, about the...the other thing." Her eyes nervously flickered around, scanning for anyone who might be able to hear. "I haven't told my mom yet. Not after... you know."

He stared at her for a long moment before swiftly nodding his head once. He made no promises or threats of leverage, but simply headed inside the kitchen.

Strangely enough, Rae wasn't worried. At least not about that. For the time being, there were more pressing matters at hand.

Chapter 15

"My dad's on his way." Luke assaulted her, and the others, with the information the second she stepped inside the kitchen the next day.

The kitchen was in vast disarray. Bits of flour, butter, and what she could only hope was cranberry juice were sprinkled all over the floor. Her friends had obviously taken it upon themselves to begin food preparations when they received the fateful news.

"Right now?" she exclaimed, her heart seizing up in her chest. "He's not supposed to get in until tomorrow! We're supposed to have a whole other day to...to..." She trailed off as her father walked into the room, flanked closely by her mother.

...to have with my dad.

Strange. She suddenly didn't have an ounce of trouble with the word.

"Wait. Your dad's coming?" Kraigan asked sharply. "Why?"

"He's coming for Thanksgiving," Molly replied in a voice much smaller than her own. "It was set up before any of...any of *this* happened."

Kraigan looked at her coldly before shrugging it away. "So, call him off. Tell him to turn back around."

"We can't," Luke said, looking miserable. "He's been looking forward to it for ages; trying to think of all sorts of reasons to drop by in the meantime to see me and Molls. Since *your* dad got here, we've been trying to put him off as best we could, but that's why he waited so long to text me." He glanced down at his phone. "He's just a few minutes away, Rae. He's not turning around."

A cold chill raced down her spine, and all the color drained out of her face.

This is it, then. This is the last time we'll all stand here together as a family. First and last.

A sardonic voice echoed in the back of her head.

Don't be silly. You'll all be in the courthouse together, too. Right before he's carted off to some Privy Council black hole and you never see him again.

"Just a few minutes?" she echoed faintly, eyes locking with Simon's.

Luke nodded sadly, looking as though he understood her plight. "Yeah, I'm sorry, Rae. I mean, we could always ask him to wait a day. Give you a little more time—"

"Time for what?" Gabriel asked sharply. Angel stood fiercely by his side.

The two of them had made it a point to steer as far away from Simon as was possible, while remaining within the confines of the house.

Rae had figured out why. The reasons for this were two-fold.

To start, there were people inside that they refused to leave unprotected. No matter how reformed Simon might claim to be, the two of them had witnessed the monster beneath more times than would allow forgiveness. As such, the best they could do was hover incessantly just out of sight, keeping a silent but lethal vigil. At any moment—ready to strike.

The other reason was that, although Gabriel might have made a tenuous vow not to take the man's life, that sort of favor was nowhere in Angel's repertoire. On three separate occasions she had attempted open violence, only to be stopped by one of the others. The fourth time, she had been caught tipping bleach into his morning drink.

Even now, Rae could see her fingers inching towards the crème brûlée torch. Julian reached down without looking and caught her by the wrist.

Rae lifted her eyes to meet Gabriel's. On the other side of the room, her mother was giving her the same look. In the end she jerked her head up and down, unable to meet her father's eyes.

They were right. The time had come to end this.

Rae sighed and then straightened and pushed her shoulders back. "Sorry about dinner, guys." Across the room she could still see Simon trying to catch her eye, but she stubbornly refused to look. "Luke, you ready to do this?"

Before he could answer Kraigan bolted forward, glaring at each of them as he positioned himself squarely in front of his father. "Ready to do what?" he demanded. "What exactly is going on?"

"We're going to turn your dear ol' daddy over to the authorities," Angel replied with a dark twinkle in her eyes. "I'm sure they have a hole in the ground somewhere with his name on it."

Simon took a shuddering step back, while Kraigan let out a vicious profanity.

"Over my dead body!"

The smile on Angel's lovely face was nothing short of terrifying. "Oh, sweetheart, I've just been waiting for you to say the word."

It was then that several things happened at once.

Kraigan lunged forward, ready to strangle her with his bare hands. Simon actually reached out to hold him back. But the second that Simon moved, Gabriel was ready.

There was an excruciating cry, then Simon was on his knees.

The screams and shouts that followed became a muffled din in Rae's ears as she stared not at her father, but at the man just seconds away from killing him. He had held out as long as he possibly could, but one wrong move and that thin layer of control had finally snapped.

Gabriel looked like some kind of avenging angel. Golden hair falling in shimmering rivulets down his face. Muscles tensed at the ready. Two raised fingers holding his enemy in place. Green eyes focused and impossibly bright. But cold. Terribly cold. With not an ounce of mercy in them.

"What?" Simon gasped, staring up at him in horror. "How are—"

"That's right, Simon," he answered in a chilling monotone. "I finally turned sixteen and got my tatù. Tell me, is it everything you'd hoped it would be? Everything you wanted?"

His fingers twitched and Simon collapsed on the floor.

The sound in the room increased, but Rae could make no sense of any of it. She could only stare, waiting for the final axe to fall. Hoping that her words would make any kind of difference.

"Gabriel," she whispered. "Stop. Don't."

There was roar of rage as Kraigan threw himself forward, shifting his murderous focus from sister to brother. If armed with any other tatù than the ones he had, it might have made a difference. But when Julian stepped in between them, bracing himself against Kraigan's thrashing fists, he came up short.

"Jules," Devon whirled around in shock, "what are you—"

"If it's Gabriel or Simon," Julian gritted his teeth with the immense strain of holding Kraigan at bay, "then I choose Gabriel."

Angel came to stand behind her brother, looking on with silent satisfaction while her boyfriend kept his attacker at arm's length. "Do it, Gabriel," she murmured in his ear. "For Jason. For Jen."

Both Beth and Simon's faces paled in identical looks of horror, while Rae looked on with utter confusion. "Who the hell is Jason?" she cried. "Gabriel, DO NOT do this!"

"Do it for us," Angel continued, gazing down at Simon's crumpled form as if she had waited a lifetime just to see it so. "Do it for Rae—she can't do it herself."

Gabriel's eyes flashed, and Simon screamed in agony once more.

"NO!" Rae shoved Kraigan aside and threw herself in between them.

Julian wouldn't lift a hand against her, even if it meant his own life. Instead, both he and Devon came together to hold her brother at bay, pinning him desperately against the wall.

"Gabriel," she grabbed his face in her hands, "we've already been over this. You're not a killer. You're not going to kill him now."

"He's not going to let himself go back to jail, Rae," he said quietly. For a split second, a flicker of genuine fear rippled across his face and he looked very much like a child. "You don't understand. It'll go wrong somehow. Something always goes wrong. He always gets away."

"He didn't," she tried to reason with him. Molly had started sneaking up behind Gabriel, hands raised at the ready, but Angel turned around to meet her head-on. "He's been locked away in that factory for almost fifteen years. He didn't escape then. He's not going to escape now."

But it was like Gabriel couldn't even hear her. He kept his eyes locked on Simon, lost in a sort of fog. One he couldn't see his way out of.

"It'll go wrong," he echoed faintly. "Something always goes wrong." He twisted his fingers up like a gun. "I have to end it."

Rae opened her mouth to scream. Felt the electricity building up in her palms.

But suddenly everything and everyone halted.

Something incredibly strange happened.

Time stopped.

It didn't freeze. It didn't slow down. It stopped. Completely.

Rae stumbled a step backwards, looking around in astonishment.

Gabriel was still frozen exactly where she'd left him. From the dilated focus in his eyes, it was clear he was beyond reason. Already, she could sense the telltale shift of power in his hands.

Behind him, Molly and Angel were locked in a miniature war. Unwilling to risk freezing the baby, Angel had snatched up a rolling pin and was bringing it down with terrifying force upon Molly's head. But Molly's eyes were electric blue, and the deadly lightning was already shooting in the air between him. Rae could make out every twisting neon strand, vibrating with a gentle hum she'd never noticed before.

On the other wall, Julian and Devon were about to lose their grip on Kraigan. They were two of the most capable people she had ever met, but it was like trying to cage a wild animal. Five bloody streaks ripped down Julian's cheek, as if Kraigan had slashed him with his nails, and despite the grip Devon had on his shoulder he was just seconds away from breaking free.

How is this happening? She rotated in a slow circle, staring around in wonder. *Am I doing this?*

Last, but not least, she came to her parents. Both kneeling, both watching the impending darkness with wide, frozen eyes. But it was something about their position that caught Rae's attention. A tiny detail that would have gone forever unnoticed if she hadn't caught it in that moment.

Simon was protecting Beth.

Despite the gut-wrenching agony of Gabriel's inescapable grasp, he had somehow managed to angle his body, so that whatever happened Beth would be spared the worst of the blow. He had no way of knowing how the power worked. That he would simply drop dead. He only thought was to contain the shockwave. To protect her from it.

Using his own broken body as a shield.

Rae had never seen anything like it. *Devon would do that for me.* The random thought threatened to catch her off-guard.

Then, before she could begin to comprehend what was happening, the edges of the room began to shimmer and dance. The frozen looks of concentration on the faces around her began vibrating with a force that she knew all too well. *Camille's kinetic energy tatù.* Yet another ability rising from within her that was beyond her control. Her body reacted in its own way. Determining what needed to be done when her brain couldn't decide what was best.

The world vibrated around here.

She tilted her head back and with a blood-curdling scream, the world came back alive.

The windows shattered. The ground began to shake. The entire room was ripped apart from the seams, spilling everyone outside onto the grass in a violent, jumbled heap.

The world went black. Then flickered on and off with bursts of color. There was a dull ringing in Rae's ears. The smell of sheetrock in the air. The taste of blood in her mouth.

She was vaguely aware that people were shifting and kicking against her, stumbling and falling as they tried to get to their feet.

A pair of strong hands grabbed her, dragging her away from the rubble.

She squinted up into the sun, expecting to see Devon, but it was her father instead. He was as pale as she'd ever seen him, and though his lips were moving she couldn't hear the sound.

Are you okay?! Sweetie, are you okay?!

Then a bright blue flashbulb froze them all in place.

With agonizing effort, Rae twisted her head to see no fewer than a dozen strangers standing on the edge of her lawn. Faces she recognized from a distance, but didn't personally know.

People from the Council. People from the school.

... People from the press?

Rae realized it was tatù press. She'd seen enough of them lingering about since everything that had happened. They'd become unwanted celebrities and she had a feeling either Kraigan's arrest, or Gabrielle and Angel's activities had left a trail right to the house.

A camera was still buzzing as the reporter slowly lowered it to his chest, gazing out in shock at the broken mansion and the battered people that had spilled out.

It seemed their little hideaway had finally been found out. But that wasn't the only secret that was soon to be exposed.

"Wait," Rae croaked, trying to speak as her father hovered anxiously above. "I can explain."

Then a final car drove up, and Luke's father stepped onto the drive. He looked in surprise at the group of people already present before gazing in downright horror at the lawn.

The pie slipped slowly from his hands.

"Simon Kerrigan..."

Rae's eyes closed as the weight of the world crashed down upon them.

"...You're under arrest."

THE END
Time Piece
Read it January 15th, 2017

Time Piece Blurb

Book #2 The Chronicles of Kerrigan Sequel

Fame is a fickle friend...

After the world discovers the infamous Simon Kerrigan is actually alive, public opinion of Rae and her friends begins to shift. While most people remain fiercely loyal, there are many who call for justice. There are even more who call for blood.

Caught in the volatile beginnings of a civil war, Rae struggles to keep the peace. But there's a battle brewing on the home front as well. As the reunited Kerrigan family gears up for the trial of a century, they all find themselves asking the same question:

Can you ever really escape the past?

Note from Author

Dear Reader:

Thanks for reading and enjoying the Chronicles of Kerrigan series!

If you're a fan, I'm going to go out on a limb and guess that you've read all 12 books of the Chronicles of Kerrigan original series. I hope you enjoyed them!

The Prequel series looks into the story of Simon and characters in the prequel will be re-introduced in the sequel!

Happy reading!

All the best, W.J. May

Newsletter: http://eepurl.com/97aYf

Website: http://www.wanitamay.yolasite.com

Facebook:
https://www.facebook.com/pages/Author-WJ-May-FAN-PAGE/141170442608149

The Chronicles of Kerrigan

Book I - *Rae of Hope* is FREE!
  Book Trailer:
  http://www.youtube.com/watch?v=gILAwXxx8MU
  Book II - *Dark Nebula*
  Book Trailer:
  http://www.youtube.com/watch?v=Ca24STi_bFM
  Book III - *House of Cards*
  Book IV - *Royal Tea*
  Book V - *Under Fire*
  Book VI - *End in Sight*
  Book VII – *Hidden Darkness*
  Book VIII – *Twisted Together*
  Book IX – *Mark of Fate*
  Book X – *Strength & Power*
  Book XI – *Last One Standing*
  BOOK XII – *Rae of Light*
  PREQUEL –
  Christmas Before the Magic
  Question the Darkness
  Into the Darkness
  Fight the Darkness
  Alone the Darkness
  Lost the Darkness

More books by W.J. May

Hidden Secrets Saga:
Download Seventh Mark part 1 For FREE
Book Trailer:
http://www.youtube.com/watch?v=Y-_vVYC1gvo

Like most teenagers, Rouge is trying to figure out who she is and what she wants to be. With little knowledge about her past, she has questions but has never tried to find the answers. Everything changes when she befriends a strangely intoxicating family. Siblings Grace and Michael, appear to have secrets which seem connected to Rouge. Her hunch is confirmed when a horrible incident occurs at an outdoor party. Rouge may be the only one who can find the answer.

An ancient journal, a Sioghra necklace and a special mark force life-altering decisions for a girl who grew up unprepared to fight for her life or others.

All secrets have a cost and Rouge's determination to find the truth can only lead to trouble...or something even more sinister.

RADIUM HALOS - THE SENSELESS SERIES
Book 1 is FREE:

Book Blurb:

Everyone needs to be a hero at one point in their life.

The small town of Elliot Lake will never be the same again.

Caught in a sudden thunderstorm, Zoe, a high school senior from Elliot Lake, and five of her friends take shelter in an abandoned uranium mine. Over the next few days, Zoe's hearing sharpens drastically, beyond what any normal human being can detect. She tells her friends, only to learn that four others have an increased sense as well. Only Kieran, the new boy from Scotland, isn't affected.

Fashioning themselves into superheroes, the group tries to stop the strange occurrences happening in their little town. Muggings, break-ins, disappearances, and murder begin to hit too close to home. It leads the team to think someone knows about their secret - someone who wants them all dead.

An incredulous group of heroes. A traitor in the midst. Some dreams are written in blood.

Courage Runs Red
The Blood Red Series
Book 1 can be downloaded at no cost.

What if courage was your only option?

When Kallie lands a college interview with the city's new hot-shot police officer, she has no idea everything in her life is about to change. The detective is young, handsome and seems to have an unnatural ability to stop the increasing local crime rate. Detective Liam's particular interest in Kallie sends her heart and head stumbling over each other.

When a raging blood feud between vampires spills into her home, Kallie gets caught in the middle. Torn between love and family loyalty she must find the courage to fight what she fears the most and possibly risk everything, even if it means dying for those she loves.

Daughter of Darkness
Victoria

Only Death Could Stop Her Now
The Daughters of Darkness is a series of female heroines who
may or may not know each other, but all have the same father,
Vlad Montour.
Victoria is a Hunter Vampire

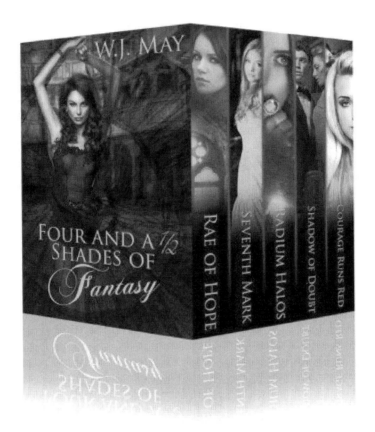

Four and a Half Shades of Fantasy

TUDOR COMPARISON:

Aumbry House—A recess to hold sacred vessels, often found in castle chapels.

Aumbry House was considered very special to hold the female students - their sacred vessels (especially Rae Kerrigan).

Joist House—A timber stretched from wall-to-wall to support floorboards.

Joist House was considered a building of support where the male students could support and help each other.

Oratory—A private chapel in a house.

Private education room in the school where the students were able to practice their gifting and improve their skills. Also used as a banquet - dance hall when needed.

Oriel—A projecting window in a wall; originally a form of porch, often of wood. The original bay windows of the Tudor period. Guilder College majority of windows were oriel.

Rae often felt her life was being watching through one of these windows. Hence the constant reference to them.

Refectory—A communal dining hall. Same termed used in Tudor times.

Scriptorium—A Medieval writing room in which scrolls were also housed.

Used for English classes and still store some of the older books from the Tudor reign (regarding tatùs).

Privy Council—Secret council and "arm of the government" similar to the CIA, etc... In Tudor times, the Privy Council was King Henry's board of advisors and helped run the country.

Don't miss out!

Click the button below and you can sign up to receive emails whenever W.J. May publishes a new book. There's no charge and no obligation.

Did you love *A Matter of Time*? Then you should read *Christmas Before the Magic* by W.J. May!

Learn how it all began ... before the magic of tatùs.

When Argyle invites his best friend, Simon Kerrigan, home for the Christmas holidays, he wants to save Simon from staying at Guilder Boarding School on his own.

Simon comes along and doesn't expect to find much more excitement in the tiny Scottish town where Argyle's family lives. Until he meets Beth, Argyle's older sister. She's beautiful, brash and clearly interested in him.

When her father warns him to stay away from her, Simon tries, but sometimes destiny has a hope of it's own.

The Chronicles of Kerrigan Prequel is the beginning of the story before Rae Kerrigan. This Christmas Novella is the start (but it may not be the end...)

The	Chronicles	of	Kerrigan	Series
Rae		of		Hope
Dark				Nebula
House		of		Cards
Royal				Tea
Under				Fire
End		in		Sight
Hidden				Darkness
Twisted Together				

Also by W.J. May

Bit-Lit Series
Lost Vampire
Cost of Blood
Price of Death

Blood Red Series
Courage Runs Red
The Night Watch
Marked by Courage
Forever Night

Daughters of Darkness: Victoria's Journey
Victoria
Huntress
Coveted (A Vampire & Paranormal Romance)
Twisted

Hidden Secrets Saga
Seventh Mark - Part 1
Seventh Mark - Part 2
Marked By Destiny
Compelled
Fate's Intervention
Chosen Three
The Hidden Secrets Saga: The Complete Series

The Chronicles of Kerrigan
Rae of Hope
Dark Nebula

House of Cards
Royal Tea
Under Fire
End in Sight
Hidden Darkness
Twisted Together
Mark of Fate
Strength & Power
Last One Standing
Rae of Light
The Chronicles of Kerrigan Box Set Books # 1 - 6

The Chronicles of Kerrigan Prequel
Christmas Before the Magic
Question the Darkness
Into the Darkness
Fight the Darkness
Alone in the Darkness
Lost in Darkness

The Chronicles of Kerrigan Sequel
A Matter of Time
Time Piece

The Hidden Secrets Saga
Seventh Mark (part 1 & 2)

The Senseless Series
Radium Halos
Radium Halos - Part 2
Nonsense

The X Files
Code X

Replica X

Standalone
Shadow of Doubt (Part 1 & 2)
Five Shades of Fantasy
Glow - A Young Adult Fantasy Sampler
Shadow of Doubt - Part 2
Four and a Half Shades of Fantasy
Full Moon
Dream Fighter
What Creeps in the Night
Forest of the Forbidden
HuNted
Arcane Forest: A Fantasy Anthology
Ancient Blood of the Vampire and Werewolf

Made in the USA
Lexington, KY
13 July 2017